"Have I been moving too fast?" Colin asked as he moved closer, but didn't touch her.

"I don't know what came over me. It's just that from the moment I saw you, you took my breath away. And you can't seem to get rid of me fast enough. I'm not used to this. I'm used to taking what I want and women don't usually put up resistance."

"That's what worries me," Noelle said. "Your reputation precedes you."

Colin moved yet closer to her. "It's just…things seem different with you. I've only known you a couple of days—and…"

"Yeah, um, right," Noelle interjected nervously.

"Have you ever wanted something so much that you go a little crazy?" Without waiting for a response, Colin tugged Noelle into his arms and held her close to his heart.

"I want something sweeter than anything else. I want to kiss you…."

Books by Candice Poarch

Kimani Romance

Sweet Southern Comfort
His Tempest

Kimani Arabesque

Family Bonds
Loving Delilah
Courage Under Fire
Lighthouse Magic
Bargain of the Heart
The Last Dance
'Tis the Season
　"A New Year; A New Beginning"
Shattered Illusions

Tender Escape
Intimate Secrets
A Mother's Touch
　"More Than Friends"
The Essence of Love
With This Kiss
Moonlight and Mistletoe
White Lightning

CANDICE POARCH

fell in love with writing stories centered around romance and families many years ago. She feels the quest for love is universal. She portrays a sense of community and mutual support in her novels.

Candice grew up in Stony Creek, Virginia, south of Richmond, but now resides in northern Virginia. This year, she and her husband will celebrate their thirtieth wedding anniversary. She is a mother of three children. A former computer systems manager, she has made writing her full-time career. Candice loves to hear from readers. Please visit her Web site at www.CandicePoarch.net or write to her at P.O. Box 291, Springfield, VA 22150.

His
TEMPEST
Candice Poarch

If you purchased this book without a cover you should be aware that this book is stolen property. It was reported as "unsold and destroyed" to the publisher, and neither the author nor the publisher has received any payment for this "stripped book."

 KIMANI PRESS™

ISBN-13: 978-0-373-86020-3
ISBN-10: 0-373-86020-X

HIS TEMPEST

Copyright © 2007 by Candice Poarch Baines

All rights reserved. The reproduction, transmission or utilization of this work in whole or in part in any form by any electronic, mechanical or other means, now known or hereafter invented, including xerography, photocopying and recording, or in any information storage or retrieval system, is forbidden without written permission. For permission please contact Kimani Press, Editorial Office, 233 Broadway, New York, NY 10279 U.S.A.

This is a work of fiction. Names, characters, places and incidents are either the product of the author's imagination or are used fictitiously, and any resemblance to actual persons, living or dead, business establishments, events or locales is entirely coincidental.

® and TM are trademarks. Trademarks indicated with ® are registered in the United States Patent and Trademark Office, the Canadian Trade Marks Office and/or other countries.

www.kimanipress.com

Printed in U.S.A.

Dear Reader,

The summer is almost here. I always look forward to less stress and more relaxation, and I hope you do, too.

His Tempest is the first of three Kimani Romance novels featuring heroines who were conceived by the use of artificial insemination. Although each character has the same donor father, their backgrounds are unique and each has a different reason for wanting to meet her donor father's family.

I hope you enjoy getting to know a hero who is struggling to keep his grandfather's share of a Thoroughbred farm in northern Virginia.

So with a tall glass of lemonade, relax in the rocker on your porch while you spend time with Colin and Noelle. Have a wonderful summer.

Warm regards,

Candice Poarch

Prologue

Any moment now, the rain would burst from the clouds.

Mackenzie Avery strolled down the sidewalk of the exclusive L.A. neighborhood in his designer jogging suit, of course—trying to blend in with the locals. He'd come here several times in the last week to see the little girl who was now pedaling her red bicycle hard, trying to make it home before the downpour began. The wind whipped her hair and clothes, but she was determined.

He snapped pictures of her with his tiny camera, which he hid when she passed him. She was close enough to touch, yet didn't recognize him. It had been four years since she'd last seen him.

He'd first seen Noelle when she'd visited her grandparents and stayed at their summer camp, which was next door to his father's thoroughbred farm in Virginia. That was when he'd fallen in love with her. He'd spent summer vacations from college at home, and her grandparents had brought the kids to his father's farm for riding lessons. Mackenzie had even taught her how to ride. But her grandparents had died four years ago and she hadn't returned since.

Mackenzie rubbed his chest as if he could rub the ache from his heart. She was his precious little girl, yet he couldn't claim her. He could never reveal to his wife or his father that he had a daughter. He'd made a promise, and if he told his father, the older man would take the next plane to California to make trouble. So he held the secret inside, and it weighed on his chest as heavy as a boulder.

Mackenzie stood in the shadows snapping pictures of the ten-year-old until she finally disappeared into the house.

If there was one thing he regretted in his life, it was not being able to participate in his daughter's life. Especially since he and his wife had just discovered that she couldn't have children. She was heartsick. And because she'd tried so hard to conceive, he was unwilling to cause her more pain.

With a sigh, Mackenzie jogged the two blocks to his car. He got in just as the clouds burst. Again he wondered if any of the other specimens he'd given had resulted in children. And if they were as healthy and as happy as Noelle. He'd never know, he realized as he drove away.

Nor would he ever return to Noelle. After all, he could never reveal to her his true identity. He'd just have to wait eight years until she came of age and then hope she'd try to contact him. That was his only chance of an introduction to his own daughter.

Chapter 1

Sixteen years later

Noelle Greenwood was late, as usual. With all the running around she had to do, what a time for her car to be in the shop! She shoved a few bills into the cab driver's hand, gathered her mountain of shopping bags and sprinted out of the car—straight into the solid wall of a man's chest. Everything went flying: packages, purse and her. She braced herself to hit the ground when strong arms captured her.

"Whoa." The man lifted her upright.

With a grateful smile, Noelle mumbled a quick "Thanks," and started shoving things back into the shopping bags.

"Let me help you with that, honey," his deep voice said. It was the "honey" that set her on edge. What right did he have to be acting so familiar? She wasn't his honey.

Noelle jerked her gaze toward the man. Not only was he attractive, he was hot, and he knew it. She was close enough to see the flecks of brown in his eyes, the sexy curve of his lips, the smooth nut-brown color of his skin. Reflexively she took a step back.

His smile beamed bright enough to melt ice. He wore black jeans on his long-legged, six-three frame, with a cream-colored sweater and a black leather jacket. The clothes molded to him in all the right places.

All that shouldn't be legal in one package, she thought.

She kept the thought to herself and gathered her things. "I have it," she said. Although she was grateful he'd saved her from landing on the street, she had things to do. Besides, men that attractive were nothing but heartache. He'd probably bumped into her deliberately. The sidewalk in front of the apartment building was wide enough for him not to invade her space. Especially since he obviously hadn't been waiting for a cab. The one she'd got out of had already pulled away from the curb, and he'd made no effort to stop it.

"I'll take care of the packages, thank you." She took the sweater dangling from his fingers and a box from his hand. "Excuse me."

The thousand-watt smile slipped. "Is everyone in Memphis this unapproachable?"

"Must be your unlucky day." She knew she was acting irrationally, but his kind brought out the worst in her.

"Guess so," he said. "If you're sure…"

"I'm positive. Thanks." With the boxes safely tucked into the bags, she scrambled to hook all the handles together and move on.

"You forgot something," he said, dangling a black lacy bra by the strap on one long finger for the entire world to see.

She grabbed the swinging bra and stuffed it into a bag. "Thank you." If she gritted her teeth any harder, she'd need a porcelain inlay.

Shaking his head, every lady's dream man finally walked off into the building. He struck her as the kind who wouldn't settle down with one woman when five would do.

Noelle rushed inside and punched the elevator button for her fifth-floor apartment. The unnerving man was nowhere to be seen. And she felt grateful.

She had her hands full with having to make nice with another man she was to meet that very afternoon. And from what she'd been told, Colin Mayes was another hottie. She had her work cut out for her. She had to talk her way into his home— without putting out, because Colin Mayes lived on the same estate as her grandfather. A grandfather who didn't know she existed.

Still puzzled over the rude woman he'd met earlier that afternoon, Colin Mayes stood beside Brent Jamison observing a much more agreeable female. She was a good hundred feet away, parading across the lawn, putting on a show as if she knew he couldn't help but stare. With a haughty glance she turned away, and Colin chuckled.

She was stunning, he thought as he looked over the sleek lines of one of the most beautiful females he'd ever laid eyes on. Long legs, a little reserved, but plenty of sass, too. And a lot of mystery. She was the kind of female that would keep a male guessing. He started to approach her, then stopped himself, as curious, she tossed her head toward him once again.

Oh, yeah. She was the one. He had to have her. He'd give anything, do anything to get her.

"She's a beauty, isn't she?" Brent said, clearly pleased.

Colin didn't respond, couldn't reply, really. He'd wanted this fine-looking filly too long to blow the deal now. He was taking a huge gamble, risking everything for her, especially considering how badly his father wanted to sell the family's half of River Oaks Thoroughbred Farm. His dad held Colin's carefree lifestyle over his head as a threat to sell River Oaks. For some time, he'd been harranging Colin about settling down. Colin had slowed down a lot, but at twenty-eight he wasn't ready to live the life of an old married man. There wasn't a female alive who could make him give up his freedom. Not yet anyway. Besides, his grandfather had left the farm in a lot of debt. What woman wanted a man who couldn't afford the bling?

He really couldn't afford to be away now, but crucial business decisions had to be made if the farm was to continue to grow. His trainer would look after things until he returned. Equestrian breeding season was beginning and Colin would be unable to leave again until July. He planned to enjoy a little play on this trip, along with the work.

Back home in Virginia he had to put up a front for his old man—but not here.

"Take a closer look," Brent said, and signaled for the stablehand to lead the sleek black-tailed filly named Maggie Girl closer to them.

Colin had checked out her temperament, ability and conformation earlier and had been satisfied with her history. She was in good condition for breeding, not too fat or too thin. Now he looked her over thoroughly from head to hoof. Afterwards, he fed her a carrot which the mare ate eagerly from his hand. "Go on, girl," Colin said, patting her on her flank before he followed Brent into his office.

Done in mahogany and a rich burgundy hue, the room was clearly a man's domain. A slew of ribbons hung on the mahogany-paneled walls. The room was as lavish as any in Brent's palatial Memphis estate.

One day River Oaks would be this lucrative, Colin thought. Still, he knew racehorses were Brent's hobby, not his livelihood.

As if reading Colin's mind, Brent announced. "I'm ready to step down from the radio." The Jamisons owned two extremely successful radio stations.

"So soon?"

"In a year. I'm ready to spend more time on the horses, and the wife wants to travel."

"You're selling the station?"

"I've gotten some compelling offers, but the kids want to keep the business. Which brings us to the point of this trade. I have some prime horses. Some are doing well at the tracks. But I need something new. And since I'm not selling the business, I don't want to shell out any more cash than I have to. It's no secret that your stallion, Diamond Spirit, is sought after for stud fees now, but with all the improvements your grandfather and George made on River Oaks, you're cash-poor."

Nobody knew that better than Colin. His dad reminded him of how far in debt they were every time he tried to convince Colin to sell the farm.

"Dally Run sired Maggie Girl," Brent continued. "She'll be a good filly to match with your stallion. And I want to match one of my mares with Diamond Spirit. Think we can negotiate a deal that's agreeable for both of us?"

The older man leaned back in his chair and clipped off the tip of his Dominican cigar as he waited for Colin's response. He took his time lighting it.

Brent's hair was styled in a short cut. He worked

out regularly in the gym in his house and it showed. He was an extremely alert as well as shrewd businessman. But Colin wasn't a novice. He'd learned a lot at his grandfather's side.

River Oaks was just getting to the point where their number-one stallion brought in a quarter of a million for each live foal. But they needed another stallion to take over after Diamond Spirit was put to pasture due to old age. He also wanted Maggie Girl, and she wasn't cheap. At the same time, Colin didn't want a cash agreement any more than Brent did.

Colin steepled his fingers beneath his chin in an effort to stop himself from rubbing his hands together. "Then let's make it happen," he said.

"He's here," Cynthia Jamison said, dropping her purse on the bar of the extraordinary entertainment room in the Jamisons' sprawling home in an upscale neighborhood north of Memphis. "Mama said Colin and Dad have been in the office for a couple of hours. I talked her into asking Colin to dinner, so you'll have time to do your magic."

"Look at me," Noelle said. "I'm so nervous, I'm acting crazy. I went out shopping today, as if I had the money to spare." The image of that annoying stranger popped unbidden into her mind for the umpteenth time that day.

"You've got to spend something on yourself. I know you want to open your grandparents' old summer camp, but don't neglect yourself," Cindy said. "I thought you'd change your mind by now, especially since your donor father is dead."

Some months before, Noelle had discovered that her mother had used a sperm donor to conceive her, and Noelle had become obsessed with finding him. After an intensive search she'd done so, had even spoken to him before he was killed in a car crash.

"Somewhere deep inside me, I still have this need to meet his father, though I can't explain why."

"Are you going to tell him who you are?"

"I don't think so. Why disrupt his life? I actually have a father who loves me. That's why this is so hard, you know." Noelle paced up and down the carpet, paying no mind to her opulent surroundings.

"Will you relax?" Cindy said. "Why are you so nervous about meeting Colin? He's just a man. One who loves women, by the way."

"If this doesn't work out, how am I going to get into River Oaks and meet George Avery?" When she had contacted her donor father in August, he'd told her his father was still alive and he wanted her to meet him, but Mackenzie Avery had died a week after they spoke, so she doubted he'd had time to tell him.

"I don't like using Colin to get an introduction."

"Just stop it," Cindy said. "We have it all planned out. When you get to Virginia, he'll introduce you to your grandfather, and then you can drop the guy. He's always dropping women when he tires of them. So what if the shoe's on the other foot for a change?" Cindy rounded the bar, filled a glass with wine, and handed it to Noelle. "Drink this. It'll relax you. Colin has a rep, and it's about time somebody took him down a peg. If we're lucky, he'll think twice about the way he treats women in the future."

"I don't want to take him on. I just want to meet Mr. Avery. I hope I won't cause any problems for your father," Noelle said.

"Don't worry about Daddy. Business is business. But this is all play."

"You're wrong there," Noelle said, sitting on the edge of the barstool. "This is strictly business."

Cindy perused Noelle's outfit critically. "You could have worn something a little more revealing, you know."

"This works." She'd chosen her outfit carefully.

It was feminine and molded to her curves without shouting, *Come here. I'm dying to impress you.*

"Maybe you're right. In that sweater, you're making sure he won't be able to keep his eyes off you."

"Let's hope he won't." Noelle had been working on this introduction for months. Although she had always planned to reopen her grandparents' summer camp, she didn't tell her parents why she'd chosen to do so now. She hoped her father wouldn't be hurt. He was one in a million. She wouldn't do anything to hurt him.

The intercom buzzed. "They're leaving the office," Gloria Jamison's voice came through loud and clear.

"Thanks, Mama." Cindy smiled at Noelle. "Pull yourself together. It's show time."

Colin and Brent had haggled for two hours before they emerged from the office, satisfied with the deal.

"You haven't met my daughter, have you?" Brent asked, walking beside him to the house.

"Haven't had the pleasure." Colin reminded himself not to get tangled with the daughter of a man with whom he was doing business, and with whom he might need to do business in the future.

"Her college friend is visiting today. She's moving to Virginia near you. Her grandparents left her some kind of children's camp. Blue Mountain Farms. Familiar with it?"

Colin certainly was. It was the boarded-up place adjacent to River Oaks. "It's been closed down for a while but someone's been working at the house lately."

"Probably her father. She wants to open it up. Turn it into some kind of summer computer camp."

Now and then Colin rode his horse near the property. The buildings looked so weather-beaten that a stiff wind might topple them over. And so neglected, as if they were waiting for someone to come along and wake them up.

"She's got a lot of work ahead of her." Colin stopped himself from checking his watch. All he wanted to do now was get back to the apartment, call George and celebrate with a stiff glass of good old Kentucky bourbon and a willing woman.

"Gloria will be disappointed if you don't join us for dinner."

Damn. Now Colin had to sit through a meal and entertain the daughter and her friend with a bunch of college talk. Probably just finished their first semester and come home thinking they were women of the world.

Colin had met with Brent several times, but he'd never met any of his four children.

The older two, he knew, worked at the radio station. When Brent retired, one of them would probably take over.

Colin had purposely chosen to stay in a Memphis apartment that Brent provided for business clients, even though Brent had offered him lodging in his home. Away from Virginia, Colin didn't have to worry about his actions being reported to his father, and Memphis had plenty of striking women. An old college buddy was taking him to some parties to meet a few of them. He'd planned to party hard for a few days, making up for having to toe the line when he returned home to his father's watchful eye.

Colin sighed inwardly. His call to George would just have to wait. So would his shot of bourbon. But he'd have to call his friend and tell him he couldn't make the parties, unless he could get away in time. He'd see how the cards played out.

"This way." Brent pointed toward the back of the house.

They entered an entertainment room where a huge plasma TV over the fireplace took center stage. A pool table stood in one area, with a pinball machine in a corner and a poker table nearby.

"That's Cindy over there." Brent pointed to the right.

Colin could see the family resemblance in the lovely female behind the bar. She had the same rich black hair as her mother, but the dark, piercing eyes were definitely Brent's. And even better, she was older than he'd thought she might be.

"Her friend Noelle is standing on the deck," Brent said.

Noelle's back was turned to them, so all Colin could see was the back of her head. Rich auburn hair, dark and mysterious.

"I'm making drinks," Cindy said. "Bourbon okay? I know you're thirsty after being cooped up in that office."

"We are that," Brent said. "Let's take a seat over here."

Colin couldn't take his eyes off Noelle. She was dressed in an off-white sweater and a slim skirt that showed an amazing pair of legs and a nicely rounded butt. He couldn't wait to see the front view. He wanted to stand there awhile and watch her, but Brent was expecting him to sit. He turned away from the enticing view.

How lucky could a man get? he asked himself. His ship had just come in, he thought, twice in one day.

"Could you hand these drinks to the men?" Cindy asked Noelle as she came inside.

"Sure." The bar was behind the sofa, and after retrieving the drinks and cocktail napkins, Noelle walked around to the other side to hand the drinks to the men. Brent was channel-surfing for a football game.

Colin stood when she approached him and she got her first glimpse of his face.

Oh my gosh. He was the man she'd crashed into earlier. Her pulse started to beat erratically. Her insides jangled with excitement and dread.

The way Cindy had talked about Colin Mayes, Noelle had expected some forty-year-old still trying to act twenty. But Colin was no more than twenty-eight or twenty-nine. And he was drop-dead gorgeous. He wore an open-neck shirt with jeans that molded to his powerful thighs. And he was staring at her as if she was a piece of steak on his plate and he loved red meat. *What should she do now?*

Suddenly he hopped back and swiped furiously at his shirtfront. Noelle glanced down at a huge wet spot. Then she looked at the glass. It was empty.

Her mind was too fuddled to determine what had happened to the other glass.

Colin frowned. "I usually like to drink my bourbon, not wear it. What did I ever do to you?" he asked. He was just as irritated with her now as she'd been with him earlier.

"I'm so sorry. I don't know how that happened." She was mortified. She swiped furiously at the wet spot with the ineffective, tiny napkin. "If you take off your shirt, I'll wash it and dry it."

"I'll get you a clean shirt," Brent said, bending to pick the other glass off the floor. "Cindy, fix us another drink. And maybe *you* should hand it to us this time," he said, chuckling and patting Noelle on the arm.

Noelle wanted to sink into the carpet, or at least leave the room. She couldn't even look at Colin. She was wearing the bra he'd dangled on his finger earlier today, and it felt hot against her breasts.

Colin removed his shirt, revealing the most amazing chest, rippling with muscles. Deliberately taunting her, he dangled the shirt on one finger just as he'd dangled her bra.

Her face burning with embarrassment, she debated whether to take it or smack him with it.

Chapter 2

In the laundry room, Noelle washed the stain out by hand and tossed the shirt into the dryer. When she passed the kitchen, Cindy handed her a tray of hors d'oeuvres.

"Can you take these with you? I have to get moving."

Puzzled, Noelle asked, "Moving where?" Cindy was supposed to take her home later.

"Didn't I tell you I have an interview with Beyoncé for the station?" When Noelle shook her head, she said, "She's giving me just a few minutes before the concert."

Suspicious, Noelle glared at her friend who was well-known for pulling fast ones. "You neglected to tell me that."

Cindy smiled innocently, and Noelle knew something was up. "Do you mind entertaining Colin for me? Keep Dad from showing him all our baby pictures, will you?"

"You better be on your way," Brent said, passing them. "Don't want to show up late and miss it. Anything with Beyoncé sells."

"Oh, Dad, you never let up. I'm not going to be late. Oh, I forgot, Mama wants you in the kitchen."

"You entertain Colin until I get back," Brent said to Noelle, carrying his drink with him as if he was going to be a while.

Cindy started out the door. "Don't worry about your ride home. I've already taken care of that." She waved a hand. "See you later."

When Noelle made it to the game room, Colin was watching the game. "Your shirt is in the dryer," she said, trying to figure out a way to fix the mess she'd gotten herself into.

Colin nodded with a weary grimace. His bourbon glass was on the table in front of him.

He frowned. "Have we met before today? Have I done something to you? I don't *think* we've met, because I would have remembered. I just want to duck in time to miss the grenade you'll probably toss at me the next time."

"A gentleman wouldn't have mentioned my clumsiness." Noelle checked the impulse to smooth her skirt.

"Well, now. I never said I was a gentleman."

Brent's shirt, she noticed, looked as good on Colin as his own had. She resisted the urge to stare and said, "Look, I admit we got off to a rocky start. And it's all my fault."

Collecting his drink, he approached her and extended his hand. "Colin Mayes. It's a pleasure to meet you, ma'am."

Noelle's hand was enveloped in his calloused and much larger one, and she found the contrast stimulating and unnerving. "Noelle Greenwood. The pleasure is mine."

He eased onto the barstool beside her as if he belonged there as comfortably as he'd belong in any space he occupied. "This is better."

They both laughed, easing the tension in Noelle's chest.

Colin swallowed a sip of his drink and enjoyed the slow, pleasant burn down his insides.

"You don't have that natural Southern accent."

"I'm a transplant from L.A. I used to visit Cindy here on some of our college breaks and decided to settle here when I graduated. My parents live in Monterey now."

"Brent tells me you're moving to Virginia."

She nodded. "I used to go to summer camp at my grandparents' place when I was young. The last summer was when I was six, but I remember it vividly. The horseback-riding, swimming in the lake, campfires and the ghost stories that scared the daylights out of me. It was wonderful. I want to bring that joy back. But my focus will be on computers and teaching the principles of investment. I want to teach teens how to analyze stocks and have them create mock portfolios."

"Computers, investments? Sounds like a lot of work and no play."

"They'll have plenty of time to play. It's a camp, after all."

The thrill in her eyes glowed like diamonds, Colin thought, making them sparkle with vitality. He knew what it was to want something so badly you could taste it. "Wow. I couldn't pick a losing stock from a winner." The truth was he never had enough money to invest. Every spare cent went back into the farm. "Pretty expensive venture. The computers alone will cost plenty."

"Brent talked the owner of a high-tech company into donating their used computers. They're updating. Their current ones already have more power than we'll need."

Colin nodded. "So when will you be moving to Virginia?"

"The end of the week. I'm driving a moving truck down."

"A moving truck?"

"With my furniture and things."

Enjoying himself, Colin leaned back in his seat. "*You're* driving it."

Put out, she tipped her head to the side. "Yeah."

Her spine stiffened and Colin played along just to see the fire in her eyes again.

"By yourself?"

She nodded, all but bristling at him. "I can drive, you know."

"Yeah, but…"

"I'm not going to bench-press the truck, just drive it." She raised her eyebrows.

Holding his hands up, Colin chuckled. "Okay, okay. Don't throw your drink at me." She looked way too pretty with her ire up. He wanted to tease her some more, but decided to forgo the bourbon on his chest again.

"So tell me about Virginia," she said, relaxing.

"I'll do better than that. I'll show you when you arrive."

"Is that a promise?"

He nodded. The mischievous tilt to her lips dazzled him. "Let's take a look at Maggie Girl." They left the house and he cupped a hand around her elbow as they walked the short distance to the barns.

"You want to ride her?" Noelle asked.

Colin grinned, unable to contain his pride of ownership of such a fine animal. "I just bought her." They passed several stalls before they reached the horse. Colin watched Noelle stroke the mare's head and wished she were stroking him.

"I'll miss her," she said. "I ride her when I'm here. Actually I exercise her."

He was watching her, not the horse. "Feel free to come to River Oaks any time you want to ride her."

Her gaze flickered to his. "Are you sure I'll be able to get in?"

"Of course."

At that moment, Brent called them to dinner.

So far so good, Noelle thought. Although Colin was still a little wary, he was beginning to loosen up. She'd seen his eyes skim her legs and her cleavage several times. So what if his gaze set her heart to racing? It was more than a passing thing.

Noelle was surprised when, an hour after dinner, Colin told her he was taking her home. They thanked Gloria for the fabulous dinner, and Colin assured Brent they'd meet the next day.

In the car an R&B station played in the background as quiet estates gave way to the dark roads to town. They drove Poplar Avenue most of the way.

The second surprise came when he told her he was staying in Brent's apartment, which shouldn't have shocked her at all. She was trying to figure out how she was going to get to see him again when he spoke.

"Since you've been here awhile, you'll know the places a guy like me would like to see."

"I'm not sure about that, since I don't know your taste."

"You can start to get to know me at dinner tomorrow night."

He doesn't waste time, Noelle thought, which worked in her favor. This was just the opening she needed.

He parked his car and they took the elevator to her apartment, but he didn't enter. "I'll pick you up at five," he said, and left for the elevator without even trying to steal a kiss.

He was smooth, Noelle thought. His unexpected actions kept a woman on her toes.

After shutting the door, she twisted the lock in place. Leaning against the solid surface, she thought of Colin, but the sight of boxes piled in the corner reminded her that her time would be better spent packing than dwelling on Colin Mayes.

Colin was thinking about Noelle so much that he almost forgot to get off the elevator on his floor. The vibes between them were strong and he wanted to explore them further. But he wasn't going to try to get her into bed quickly. After all, she was going to Virginia, so he'd have plenty of time. But she was a friend of Brent's family. That alone was enough to keep her off his list of available women. Relationships never lasted anyway. But friendships, well, they could last.

It was all such a shame because he really wanted to know if the excitement he felt was nothing more than a quick flash in the pan or something that would flower out into a beautiful bloom.

Colin sighed regretfully and took out his key to open the door.

The red message light on the phone was blinking. George had called him five times. It was ten Memphis time, eleven Eastern Standard Time, but he knew the old man would still be up. He rarely slept more than three or four hours.

Since his son's death, George Avery took little interest in River Oaks, which he now owned with Colin's father. Colin hoped the acquisition of a new filly would lift his spirits somewhat.

"Took you long enough to call," George said when he answered, as if he'd been waiting by the phone. "How did it go?"

"We got the deal we were hoping for."

Colin could almost picture the man's terse nod before he proceeded to grill Colin on every last detail.

"What took you so long getting back?"

"Brent and Gloria invited me to dinner. Then I had to drop a guest off home."

"Your father called. Wanted to know what was happening."

Colin couldn't get any peace even when he was out of town. "I'll call him first thing tomorrow."

"When are you coming back?"

"Four or five days."

"You toe the straight and narrow. I'm not in the mood for a new partner." Then he sighed. "Whatever happens you'll still be manager of the place." They disconnected. But Colin didn't want to be just the foreman. He didn't want to work with new owners, either. An owner could make decisions a manager couldn't. As much as his dad stayed on his back, he allowed Colin to make the decisions.

His dad hounded him about everything, including settling down and getting married. Images of Noelle flashed in his mind. He saw her as a wife, a mother. She was the one woman who—*whoa. You've only been with her a few hours,* he told himself. *Come tomorrow evening you'll probably have a totally different perspective.*

But something deep in his gut told him he wouldn't. Noelle was real. She was the kind of woman he stayed away from. She was a woman he couldn't keep his mind off.

Colin arrived at Noelle's apartment at five sharp the next afternoon. He'd been so eager to be with her again, he'd counted the hours and kept wondering why. Then he gave up. She was ready—for something and so was he. But ready for what? No complications. Not now.

And although she was dressed casually in jeans with a pretty green sweater, she was every bit as astonishing as she'd been the day before. He couldn't fathom it. A friend had told him love would hit him that way. But this wasn't love, he told himself. It was lust, pure and simple. He understood lust.

"You're going to have to get rid of that jacket if you don't want barbecue sauce on it," Noelle said.

"So it's ribs."

"The best ribs you've ever wrapped your lips around. We're going to Neely's."

"Well, lead the way, ma'am."

She directed him to Neely's and in no time they were both greasy with sauce that was so delicious Noelle always had to diet for two days after going there. She only hoped there was a good rib place in Virginia.

"Tell me about your farm. How long have you worked there?"

"I don't own it personally. My father owns half, now that my grandfather is gone. He owned half the farm and his friend of many years, George Avery, owns the other half. At one time the Avery family owned the whole thing until my grandfather bought half of it. Racing was always in his blood. He's originally from horse country in Kentucky and worked with horses to help pay for college."

They finished their meal and drove along the

picturesque Riverside Drive, then sat near the Church by the River and watched boats go by.

"There was a yellow fever epidemic in 1807 that killed most of the people in Memphis. The black burial ground is here." They sat quietly for several moments thinking of the devastation. It was still, and winter birds soared across the horizon.

Soon evening slipped in and they walked along Beale Street. Lively blues music was seeping out of the doors of several brightly lit clubs, still, peace settled over Colin. He glanced at Noelle. Her hair was windblown, her face fresh and lively. He was amazed at how much he was enjoying himself.

Then his cell phone rang and he glanced at the number. His dad.

"George told me about the horse you bought," Leander Mayes jumped right in. "You didn't get my permission to pay good money for a mare."

"We did a trade. A no-cash deal."

"Well, you should have informed me before you made the trip."

"You were out of town. Besides, I didn't think you were interested."

"I am where finances are concerned."

"Dad, why don't you let George and me run the—" Colin had to hold the phone from his ear while his dad fussed for a good three minutes before he disconnected.

"Want a drink?" Colin asked Noelle then. "I need one if you don't."

"Sure." Noelle hoped he wasn't in the habit of drinking his problems away. "Do you realize your phone and ring tone are just like mine?"

"You're kidding. Maybe one of us should change the ring or you might end up answering my phone."

They slipped into a club where a blues band was playing. A woman with a huge voice was belting out a sad ballad. After asking Noelle her beverage preference, Colin ordered bourbon for himself and a club soda with lime for her. They listened to the music of struggle and heartbreak, which seemed to send Colin deeper into the shadows that consumed him.

Noelle watched the play of lights across his face, wishing she could calm the storm raging in his mind. But some things a man had to mull over before he settled on a solution.

They had been so lighthearted before, and now...

"How did you get involved in the farm?" Noelle asked when she thought Colin had contemplated long enough.

He scooted his chair closer to hers. "I started

right after Grandpa bought in. I used to spend summers with him and some weekends. He put me to work right away, and I grew to love it. After I left school I bummed around a bit. Worked at the farm some for a year, then Granddad convinced me to go to college for a degree in equestrian science. Which I did." He shrugged. "I graduated four years ago and returned to the farm. Granddad died two years after that. The farm was sinking pretty fast, except he and George had a stud whose offspring have been doing pretty well at the track. So we're slowly pulling out of debt."

"You're going to make it, you know that?"

"Even I know wishing doesn't make it happen."

"No, but you have to start somewhere. And I've got a good feeling about you."

For the first time since they entered the club, his eyes brightened. "You know, you're good for me."

"Am I?" She didn't know if it was him or the drink talking. Still, she couldn't deny that she understood where he was coming from. She was striking off across country to follow a dream.

She took his hand in hers and caressed it. There were layers to him she hadn't begun to unravel.

"Surely your father knows what this farm means to you."

He shrugged, giving her a sheepish glance. "I haven't exactly lived the life of a saint."

"What young man has?"

"You've got a point there. I like you, Noelle Greenwood."

Without asking he pulled her onto the dance floor. They danced and listened to the music for an hour before they made it back to the car and he drove home.

He'd planned to leave her at the door just as he had the night before. But, awareness had shimmered in the air all evening, and when the door closed behind them, it was as if they'd been given permission to surrender to their deep-seated desire. The moment Colin's lips touched hers he felt as if a sunburst had exploded through his body. It shook him to the core. For a brief second he wondered if the same thing had happened to her. He drew his tongue over the seams of her lips and she opened to him like a flower spreading its petals to the sun.

"So sweet," he whispered. Then he dipped his tongue into her mouth. Her moan opened the gates to the swell of emotions welling up inside him. He pressed her closer to him and ground his hips against hers. Their tongues dueled until he probed again. A feast was spread before him, yet he couldn't get enough to fill him.

It was crazy, Noelle thought. It was wild. What she felt was unlike anything she'd ever felt before.

The trail of Colin's finger on her cheek was intimate and unnerving. She smiled at him and he lowered his head and captured her lips once again. Time stood still as they lost themselves in new and exciting emotions.

When she felt his hands on her breasts, reason reasserted itself. "We can't," she said on a shaky breath. "I don't know you."

"You know my hopes and dreams. You know everything that's important," he said as his lips grazed hers.

Noelle had never even contemplated going to bed with him. Especially after seeing him just twice. That wasn't like her. She heard Cindy's warning echo in her mind. But it was hard to listen to when desire was speaking louder. She knew she was just another notch on his belt. But what a notch he was!

Leaning her head against his chest, she closed her eyes tightly. She couldn't do this.

He must have felt it the moment she'd changed

her mind because he leaned against the door with his hands aligned against the surface, his body was still pressed against hers. She knew how very much he wanted her, and how much she wanted him. Her hands were still gripping him.

"Okay, okay." He swiped a hand across his face, tried to think logically. He knew it was too soon for intimacy, but his brain wasn't doing the talking right now.

Colin looked down at the woman to whom he was molded. She might be saying no with her mouth, but she was still clutching him. What on earth did she think he was made of? Stone?

She was staring up at him now as if she didn't know where to take it from there. He blew out a long breath, willed his heartbeat to slow down.

"I hadn't planned to jump you as soon as you got home. I'd planned maybe a movie, conversation, you know, a get-to-know-you-better kind of thing. My senses just seem to leave me whenever we're together."

He had to keep reminding himself that she was more than a quick turn in the sheets. He would have had her against that door in a second, entered her and had his fill of her, but it wasn't right.

He bent and kissed her sweet lips once again.

Hers were warm and slightly trembling. He loved their dewy softness, he basked in her response to him. This softness he felt for her was new.

He eased back from her and pulled her to the sofa where they sat like two teenagers with their parents in the next room. They looked at each other and laughed, easing the tension, if not the desire.

"So what are your plans for tomorrow? Are you working?" he asked.

She shook her head. "No. I've already quit my job. I'm packing for the trip. My brother is coming in a couple of days to help pack the truck and drive with me to Virginia."

"I have work tomorrow, but how about I come by tomorrow night, and the next day I'll help you pack?"

She hesitated. "Things are moving too fast between us."

"I'm just offering to pack. We can drive back together. It'll be a caravan...sort of. I'm driving Maggie Girl back as soon as things are finalized. And I'm taking Brent's mare also."

"Did you see Maggie Girl today?" Noelle asked.

"Oh, yeah." Brent chuckled. "We spent some time together. She's going to love it in Virginia with Diamond Spirit."

Exhaling a long breath, Noelle finally relaxed. "Horse lovers are something else."

"You think so?"

"I know so." He looked so sure of himself and so smug, Noelle shook her head.

"And I know you're entirely too enticing." With that, he stood up. "I'd better go before I end up making a fool of myself." Without another word, he was out the door.

Chapter 3

Noelle was definitely curious. Colin seemed nothing like the man Cindy had described. She'd wanted him every bit as much as he wanted her. Not that she thought he was a saint by any stretch of the imagination, but he wasn't quite the ladykiller, either.

Too full of energy to sleep, she changed her clothes and was knee-deep in packing when the phone rang.

"How did it go?" Cindy asked.

Feeling foolish for her emotions for Colin, Noelle cleared her throat. She wasn't supposed to feel anything. This was a business deal, but her thoughts weren't listening to logic. "Fine, I guess." It had been well over a year since her last serious date and she wasn't ready to be brought back to reality.

"The way he was undressing you with his eyes, that's all you have to say?"

"I guess it went better than I thought. Only I'm a little worried." Noelle paused, wondering how much she should reveal. But Cindy was her friend, and she had a better feel for Colin. As a reporter, she read people more easily than Noelle did.

"I think he really has feelings for me."

Cindy laughed.

Noelle couldn't believe the hussy was laughing at her. Friend or not, she wanted to hit her.

"I knew it," Cindy said. "I just knew you'd be taken in. He's got a long history of lovin' and leavin'. Don't let his games fool you into bed. He's a player, girl. A champion at games."

Feeling increasingly uncomfortable, Noelle wished she'd kept her mouth shut. "I've been around enough players to know when someone is insincere."

"There are players and there are *players*. Colin falls into the second category."

"I think you're wrong this time. This is the first

time you've met him. You're judging him by rumors. He seems so real."

"There's usually a grain of truth in rumors." Then Cindy's voice softened. "And good actors always seem real. Look. You're a smart woman. You graduated at the top of your class. Don't be a fool in the game of life," she rambled on undaunted. "You get what you need out of him, and then tell him goodbye. And don't let him get in your panties in the meantime, you hear?"

Noelle's long sigh must have carried over the line.

"Trust me. He's run a line on a whole string of women, leaving heartbreak from Kentucky to Virginia. I don't want you to be one of them."

Noelle wanted to relieve the concern in her friend's voice. "He just seemed so...so genuine."

"Part of the game, girlfriend. So get to know him well enough for him to invite you to the farm and introduce you to your grandfather."

"All right. You've convinced me. I'll keep my guard up." Noelle sighed and sat at the kitchen table. "Oh, Cindy. This is such a mess. I hope Dad doesn't think I don't love him or feel betrayed when he finds out."

"He doesn't have to know."

From the time Noelle had found out she was the

product of artificial insemination, she'd been eager to meet her donor father and his family. She'd tried to make herself believe it was for medical purposes—needing to know his medical history so she'd know what to expect for herself and for the children she'd have one day. The truth was she wanted to see him face to face.

Her donor father, Mackenzie Avery, had agreed that she could contact him once she reached eighteen. Her relationship with her father was great and she felt as though she was betraying him by wanting to meet her donor father, so she'd waited until recently to contact him.

But the week after they'd spoken on the phone, Mackenzie had died. That was six months ago. He'd told her they'd met when she was a child and spent summers at her grandparents' summer camp. He'd given her riding lessons and she'd visited his veterinary office. Noelle vaguely remembered him. Not his face, but she remembered the gentle man who gave her lessons and the thrill of being in his office.

"Mackenzie seemed so nice when I talked to him. I wish I'd gotten the chance to meet him." He'd promised to visit her, but had died before he'd had the chance.

Mackenzie's father, George Avery, was still

alive, though, and lived in Virginia. At least she could meet him.

Noelle wondered again if she even needed to go through this charade. Deep down, she sensed someone was going to get hurt. Whenever she used deception, it always backfired. "I still think I should have gone to Virginia and tried to meet him on my own. I shouldn't involve anyone else."

"My dad knows the family," Cindy said. "He went to Mackenzie's funeral. I asked him questions about George Avery. They have a prize stallion, and they get a hundred grand every time he covers a mare. You better believe they guard that farm like Fort Knox. And after his son's death, Mr. Avery doesn't go out often. So this is the best way."

"Still grieving, I'm sure," Noelle murmured. "It has to be devastating to lose your only child. Maybe his family can give him some solace."

"My dad told me he has a sister and some nephews and nieces who live in other states," Cindy murmured. "So that's it, except for you, kiddo. Mackenzie never had other children. He and his wife divorced about three years ago. They sold the house and he moved back into the family home with his dad."

"Well, thanks for talking your dad into using their stud for his prized mare."

"It gave me practice for when I ask for a promotion and a raise. I learned some new skills negotiating that deal."

"Thank you anyway."

"So have you and Colin made any plans to see each other again?"

"He's going to help me pack."

"You don't fool around, do you?"

"No, he doesn't fool around."

Cindy's tone turned serious again. "I'll call you tomorrow. And remember, it's all a game to Colin. You're just his entertainment. He'll forget you as soon as he leaves the city."

"I'll remember."

Cindy was probably right, Noelle thought when she hung up. Noelle was always willing to give people the benefit of doubt, but her heart had been broken numerous times. This time she'd make sure her guard was up when she was with Colin because he was too convincing.

The kiss entered her mind again and this time she deliberately banished it. She had too much packing to do to think about Colin, and she worried about her dad finding out the main reason for her trip.

Franklin Greenwood was a great father. The fact that she wanted to meet her donor father wasn't a reflection on him. She was the apple of his eye, and she knew it. She'd never deliberately hurt him. He'd questioned why she wanted to move to Virginia, and somehow she didn't think the summer camp was a convincing reason.

She didn't usually lie to him—hadn't until now. And that didn't sit well with her. But she didn't know how to handle it any other way.

Never in his entire life had Colin met a woman who had had such a devastating impact on him.

It frightened the heck out of him.

When he woke the next morning, he felt foolish. He was pursuing her the way he went after the flavor-of-the-month. And she was nothing like that. She was serious—the kind of serious he usually avoided. He didn't understand this constant need to pursue her.

It was daylight when he got dressed, then he went to the Jamisons'. The grooms were already mucking out the stalls. He saddled Maggie Girl and led her out of the stable. Riding usually cleared his head.

After a walk, Colin urged the mare into a brisk trot. The cool winter air whipped against him.

It was going to take a little persuading to get

back into Noelle's good graces. She was already skeptical of him, he thought, as he considered his next move. For a moment he wondered why he was going to the trouble. His only explanation was some magnetic force that seemed to pull him to her. Except, that made no sense at all.

He rode for nearly half an hour, letting his mind clear of everything except the pleasure of the ride before he brought Maggie girl back to the stables and cooled her down. Then he brushed her before he left.

Roses. A huge pot of them greeted Noelle when she opened her door. Beneath the roses was a pair of legs. All she could see were legs and roses.

Then a hand slipped around the huge bundle to reveal a white bag whose enticing aroma mixed with the fragrance of the roses. "Breakfast," Colin said. She had yet to see his face.

Noelle laughed.

Smiling, Colin came into the room and placed the vase of flowers on the table.

"What did I do to deserve all this?" Noelle asked, still standing near the door.

"Look. I moved a little fast yesterday. I admit it. I don't know what came over me. It's just..." He walked closer to her, but not close enough to touch her. "From the moment I saw you, you took my breath away, even on that first day when you couldn't get rid of me fast enough in front of the building. I'm used to taking what I want and women don't usually put up resistance."

"That's what worries me," Noelle said. "Your reputation precedes you."

He sighed. "I know. It's just...things seem different with you. I don't know what's come over me. I've only known you a couple of days..."

"Right."

"Have you ever wanted something so much that you act a little crazy?" he asked.

"Like the way you feel about your horses?"

He chuckled. "I wouldn't quite put you in the same category as I would my horses."

She cocked an eyebrow. "A close runner-up, maybe?"

"Not even close." He still held the bag in his hand. "I came with gifts. First I feed you, then I work." He closed the distance between them and held the bag out.

But she still wasn't quite ready to take a step with him. "Don't think the most gorgeous arrangement of roses I've ever seen and breakfast is going to change my opinion of you."

The cheeky grin he revealed was enough to make her run screaming in the opposite direction.

"I hope you'll get to know me and then you'll see I'm a good guy after all. We're going to be neighbors. I want to make a good impression."

Shaking her head, Noelle took the bag from his hand. With that look he could melt snow. "If you're trying to impress me, it's working." Unable to resist the enticing smells, she opened the bag. "How did you know I was starved?"

"Calculated guess."

She couldn't stand his scrutiny any longer. She regarded the lavish arrangement. "Oh, my gosh. The roses."

She didn't know how he kept from stumbling over boxes. What an apology. She was being drawn into Colin's spell.

He moved the vase of flowers to the center of the table. Noelle leaned over and smelled the petals. They actually had an aroma that was often missing from the hothouse variety.

"You didn't get these from the local supermarket."

"Nope. I wanted to make sure you didn't toss them back at me." His grin was enticing. "So, breakfast, then work?"

Noelle thought she'd sorted things out as far as

Colin was concerned. And then he sprang this on her. If this was just an act he was good enough to win an Oscar. But suddenly he leaned close and kissed her. "I know it sounds trite, but no woman has ever appealed to me the way you have—especially not so quickly. I'll be the first to say I'm a ladies' man. But with you, it's all different."

Colin couldn't believe he was baring his soul this way, and what he spoke was the truth. He tugged Noelle into his arms and held her close to his heart.

"I want something sweeter than breakfast."

"You're undoing what you've accomplished so far."

"I know. But I want to kiss you. Just one kiss. That's all."

He felt her hesitate. "That's what they all say."

He spread his fingers through her heavy hair and smoothed it back. He tilted her head so that her lips were positioned for him.

"Just one kiss," he whispered again. "I won't take it any further. Promise."

And then he kissed her. She tasted so sweet, all thought rushed out of his mind, and he lost himself in the emotions of the moment until the sound of a car horn passing on the street brought him back to reality.

Suddenly he pulled away from her. He gazed at her, wanting to imprint her in his memory. Her breath was as ragged as his. Her lips were slightly swollen and moist, her breasts rose and fell with each breath.

He swiped a hand across his face. "Tell you what. I'll start packing while you eat."

Noelle was in trouble. If she was this heated up over a simple kiss, what would her reaction be if they took it to another level? As unwise as even the kiss had been, she was definitely curious. Maybe they were moving too fast, but he seemed every bit the skilled man Cindy had described.

When Noelle opened her door two days later, she was shocked to see her brother and father standing there. She'd known her brother was coming, but her father's presence was a complete surprise.

"What are you doing here?" Noelle asked, pleased to see him.

Her dad enveloped her in one of his big bear hugs. He was a tall, lean, broad-shouldered man who loved to play golf, which was one of the reasons he and her mother had moved to Monterey. He watched Tiger Woods play at Pebble Beach every time he came.

"Had to come and see you off. How are you?" Franklin Greenwood asked.

"Okay." Angst ate at her insides. She needed to tell him the truth, but she feared he wouldn't understand. Up till now they'd shared everything, and her deception weighed heavily on her heart.

"Well, now. Is there still a bed for me to sleep in?" her dad said.

"Of course." She stepped back from him and hugged her brother, Greg. "Come on in." Her brother took his duffel bag to the spare bedroom, but her dad stopped as soon as he crossed the threshold and saw Colin taping up a box.

Colin approached her father and extended a hand.

"Dad, this is Colin Mayes. He lives next door to Blue Mountain Farms."

Her father shook his hand.

"How do you do, sir," Colin said.

Her father nodded. "You're George's grandson?"

"No. My grandfather was his partner."

"He's here buying one of Brent's horses," Noelle said to break the strained atmosphere.

Franklin nodded again. "I just came back from Virginia."

"I didn't know you were going there," Noelle said.

"Wanted to check on the work you had done on the house." He shook his head. "You've got your work cut out for you."

"I know. Had they finished the wiring?"

"Yes. I replaced a couple of broken windows, put in a new heating system and furnace. I scrubbed the walls and floors, aired it out. Greg and you will have to paint before you move the furniture in. But at least it's livable."

"Thanks, Dad, but I was going to do all that."

"Baby, I've got to be able to sleep nights. And if I had to worry about you being in a cold, unsafe house, it wasn't going to happen. Besides, you still have the camp to repair. It'll keep you busy."

"What shape is the camp in?"

"Worse than the house. But I knew you had to do it."

He knew about Mackenzie Avery, Noelle realized just then, but she wasn't ready to broach that subject just yet.

Her father hefted his duffel. "Well, I'm going to put this in back and we'll get to work."

Colin came up beside her. "I don't think your father likes me."

"He'll come around."

"I don't know. I didn't make the best impression on him. I wasn't mentally prepared to meet your father."

"We'll see." According to Cindy, Colin was

every father's worse nightmare. But when he closed the distance between them, the temperature in the room seemed to increase by sixty degrees. Colin tugged her to him, and the intensity of his gaze darkened. As much as Noelle tried to make herself believe Colin was deceptive, her heart wasn't listening. The room sizzled and crackled with sexual tension.

Tilting her chin, he lowered his head and kissed her. She wanted to fight the heat zinging through her body, but she was helpless against his potency. His mouth was warm and seductive, sending points of desire through her system. At that moment her entire world was centered on him. And by the time he released her, she knew she was in trouble.

He was regarding her with his trademark tilted smile. When she looked at that smile—when she gazed into his eyes—she believed they could last. Believed that in his eyes, she was the only woman alive. Believed he would never look at another woman again in the same way he was gazing at her.

As much as she wanted to share something deeper with him, she knew they weren't going to last. And that made her sad.

* * *

That night Noelle still hadn't broached the subject of Mackenzie Avery. She touched her father's arm. Her brother was in bed and she and her dad were sitting on the couch watching the late news.

"Dad, I need to talk to you. I should have said something before now."

He turned from the news and focused on her. "I know."

"Although it's been my lifelong dream to open Blue Mountain Farms, I have two reasons for going there."

"You've wanted to be a part of that camp from the time you were little. It's the reason your grandparents left it to you."

Noelle realized he didn't want to broach the real subject any more than she did. Could he be as afraid of losing her as she was of losing him?

"Do what you have to do, okay? Seek what you have to seek."

Her throat felt as dry as cotton. "Daddy?"

His smile warmed her in a way that melted her heart. "What is it, sweetheart?"

She tried to speak but the words caught in her chest. Tears clogged her throat, but she had to tell him.

"I contacted him." She didn't need to say who *him* was.

Her father nodded.

"I just…"

He gathered her into his strong arms. She used to think he could solve all her problems, handle any situation. She'd always been Daddy's girl. There were times they'd sat on the steps of their home and weeded through any problems, her concerns floating away as gently as a summer breeze. She wasn't a little girl any longer, yet, she still needed him. Still needed to smell the subtle scent of his familiar cologne. Still needed to reaffirm he was her dad and her world hadn't changed.

"I…I love you," she finally said, not knowing what else to say.

"Honey, I know that. I love you, too." He leaned back and lifted her chin with his thumb. Wiping the tears from her eyes, he said, "Nothing will ever come between us."

Noelle closed her eyes again and found herself enveloped in his arms. She wrapped her arms tightly around him as if she'd never let him go.

Noelle stood by the truck at the Jamison place two days later, waiting for Colin and the Jamisons' general manager to finish loading the horses into the trailer. Her brother and dad had packed her moving truck and hitched her car to the back.

All that was left now was to say goodbye. She'd been emotional all morning, not knowing what to say to her father.

Finally, she just hugged him. When she pulled away, she wiped her eyes with the back of her hands.

Franklin dug into his pocket for his wallet, as if she were a teenager. "Need some money?"

Noelle laughed. "No, Dad. I have enough."

"I need money," Greg said, coming around the corner eating one of the sandwiches Gloria's cook had prepared for them to take on the trip.

"When don't you need money?" Her dad pulled out several bills and thrust them into Noelle's hands even with her objections. He seemed to need to complete that fatherly act, so she accepted with a hug. Then he handed money to his son.

His real son, Noelle thought.

But she was his real daughter in every way that counted.

Noelle was closer to meeting her grandfather, closer to seeing photographs of her natural father, learning about the man he'd been. She wondered what he'd looked like, if her hair was like his. Or her eyes, her nose.

They started out on 40 East, which ran into 81 North, Colin and the trailer behind them the whole way. Though the view of the Blue Ridge Mountains was breathtaking, she was glad her brother was there to help with the long hours of driving.

They were halfway through the trip and Noelle was resting in the passenger seat when Greg asked, "Does Mom know why you're really moving there?"

"I'm sure she and Dad discussed it."

"This year you're going to be busy repairing everything at the camp, but after this summer, you'll have nothing to do for the rest of the year."

"I'll figure out something. I can always teach computer classes to make ends meet, and my old job will let me work a few months." The computer company she'd worked for would allow her to telecommute. "The summer camp seemed to take care of Grandma and Grandpa."

"That's because they were both teachers. I still wonder why after teaching all year, they'd want to babysit kids during the summer."

"They loved kids. They only had one camp session each summer, remember?"

"I was too young. You're the one who did the

summer-camp thing. That's why they left me the cave. Think I'll take a look while we're here. So what's up with you and Colin? Is it serious?"

"Don't pull out the suit. I've only known him a week."

"Hmm. Y'all were looking pretty tight."

Noelle shrugged. She couldn't name what they shared and didn't even try.

She was grateful for the next fill-up stop to avoid her brother's probing questions. And because she and Colin got to spend a few minutes together. She felt herself falling for him in a dangerous way. No matter what Cindy said, Noelle didn't think a man could fake emotions this intense. At least she wanted to think better of Colin.

Around eight that evening, they made it to Front Royal, Virginia, less than an hour's drive to her new home. While Colin drove the horses home, Noelle and her brother stopped at a hotel. After the long drive she wasn't up for rolling out sleeping bags in the house and spending the night on a hard, dusty floor. Besides, after her father's assessment, she'd rather get her first glimpse of the place in daylight.

It was late when Colin called her.

"Got the horses settled in?" she asked.

"Yeah."

"How is Mr. Avery?" Colin had talked about him during their time in Memphis so she felt comfortable in bringing him up.

"Great. He came out to the barns. He likes Maggie Girl. I told him all about you. He was friends with your grandparents and is looking forward to meeting you."

Noelle swallowed her anxiety. "I'm looking forward to meeting him, too."

He sighed. "Noelle, I'm falling for you in a way I never expected. I mean, we've been together less than a week, yet we've spent so much time together it seems as if we've known each other much longer."

"I feel the same."

"I don't know where this is taking us. It's so new and— I don't know. I haven't been serious about one woman in years.... I can't promise you anything. I don't know the future of the farm."

Her heart beat erratically in her chest. "I'm not asking for anything."

"But women like men who have a promising future. And everything for me is up in the air. But I love what I do. If I didn't, I'd get a regular nine-to-five job so that I could buy you jewels and the biggest house and—"

"I'm not asking for anything. My future is just as iffy as yours. I gave up a great job to drive halfway across the country to start a summer camp that hasn't been open in twenty years. So I guess we're starting from the same place."

"You're special, you know that?"

Oh God, oh God. What have I gotten myself into? After the days they'd spent sightseeing, she thought he'd be ready to move on by now. She'd deceived him and now he was baring his soul to her. She had to come clean.

"Colin, when we met, I never expected—"

"I know. I never thought we'd get this far, either. But all this can't be one-sided. You feel it, too, don't you?"

"Yes, but—"

"Give me a chance, okay? Give *us* a chance. That's all I'm asking. I want a chance to see where this leads. I want to get to know you better."

Noelle closed her eyes on the emotions lapping over her like the rippling warm waters of a whirlpool. She wanted to move forward with him, too. "Okay," she whispered.

Chapter 4

The workday began early on a thoroughbred farm. At quarter to five Colin was out of bed. A half hour later he was downstairs, where the housekeeper, Leila Nelson, was already in the kitchen preparing breakfast, and looking much too fresh for so early in the morning. Her hair was neatly pinned up and, as usual, she wore a dress, a blue one this morning. Colin couldn't ever remember seeing her in a pair of slacks.

The brown-skinned woman glanced up and smiled. "Welcome home," she said. "I stayed up as long as I could last night, but you got in very late.

Left supper in the fridge for you, but you didn't touch it."

"After unloading the horses, I went straight to bed. How's George?"

"Moping around. I couldn't convince him to go to the grief session at church. Maybe he'll listen to you."

Disappointed, Colin said, "I'll take him with me to the track this morning. We have three yearlings that will start racing soon."

"Good. He needs to get out," she said, setting a plate of pancakes before him.

After the delicious breakfast, Colin made his way to the barn, where they were preparing some of the horses for the practice track.

Thinking of Noelle, as he always did lately, he dialed her cell number. She'd asked him to call her early, but he wondered if she'd appreciate being awakened this early.

She cleared her throat before uttering a sleepy, "Hello."

"Half the morning's gone. What're you still doing in bed?" Colin asked.

"What?"

He grinned. "This is your wake-up call."

"Oh, hi." She moaned and the sound shot heat right through Colin's groin. There was something sexy about a woman's sluggish morning voice. "It's still dark. It can't be morning yet."

"Sure it is. Now, if you were home I could ride my horse over there and wake you gently and slowly. You'd only be a mile away. But this is the best I can do from here."

"You're only a mile from my grandparents' house?"

"Less than that by horseback." He heard the mattress groan when she moved. He'd give anything to be in that bed snuggled up close with her right now. He felt his body react at the thought. He tightened his hand around the phone.

"It'll be late before I can get away to see you. Got a long day ahead of me."

"Yeah, me, too. Thanks for the wake-up."

"Anytime, sweetheart." Sighing, he closed his phone, tossed his diposable cup in the trash and entered the barn where the groom was already at work preparing the horses to board the trailer for the short ride to the practice track.

Colin wanted to keep George too busy to sit around the house grieving.

Within that one week Colin had been away, George had lost weight, adding to the total he'd lost since Mackenzie's death.

Although Colin respected the grieving process, he wanted to help George. And the best way, he figured, was to get him involved in an activity he loved.

The sun hadn't quite broken the horizon when they left the farm. Frost was still on the ground when they arrived at the track.

Colin went to get more coffee for them. He handed one cup to George. "So what do you think of Maggie Girl?"

"Good choice."

When George failed to mention any of the characteristics that made a prime thoroughbred, Colin changed the subject.

"Do you remember the Eppses on Blue Mountain Farms?" he asked. "They used to run a summer camp."

George nodded.

"Their granddaughter is here. She's opening the camp."

"Those buildings need work."

"She's having them repaired."

"Where's she going to stay?"

"In the house. Her dad had some work done to make it livable."

"He stopped by when he was here. The family came to Mackenzie's funeral."

Colin didn't remember. So many people had attended. "The granddaughter's name is Noelle. I want you to meet her. I saw a lot of her in Memphis. Her brother is here for the week to help her settle in before he returns to school."

"You like her?" George asked, never taking his eyes off the activity around them.

"Yes."

"Is she different from the rest? Her grandparents were friends with my wife and me."

Colin focused on the racetrack where jockeys and trainers were preparing for the race. "She's special."

"Why don't you invite them to dinner?" George nodded toward Colin's shirt pocket. "Use that fancy phone of yours and call Leila." George hadn't caught on to cell phones yet.

"I'll do that."

George sipped his coffee and looked out toward the track. "Be good to have company again. Leila likes to entertain. Been complaining nobody's been over lately."

This was a good sign, Colin thought. A very good sign. He'd have Noelle and her brother over if he had to drag them kicking and screaming. But with Noelle's soft heart, she'd readily agree.

***

Noelle was still basking in her call from Colin when daylight broke over the horizon. She and her brother drove past the camp entrance and a half mile later turned onto the graveled path that led to her grandparents' home. She dodged huge potholes, small branches and patches of weeds. The trees were thick and plentiful, but it was easy to see through the bare branches. They entered a clearing and she got her first glimpse of the old Colonial-style house. What used to be white had now weathered gray with age.

"This place is begging for paint," Gregory said from the passenger seat.

"At least it has good bones," Noelle said. "You're offering to paint the outside?"

"If I had another month or two."

Four columns supporting the wide front porch stood tall and strong.

Noelle remembered sitting in a rocker with a glass of juice. An old rusty glider was still there, pushed to the side. It had been sitting on that front porch in rain, snow, heat and hail for years.

Nostalgia carried Noelle back a couple of decades, and a lump formed in her throat. "Do you remember summers here?"

"A little, not much."

"You're too young," she said. "See that pecan tree over there? Grandpa made a rope swing on it. It was the best swing I ever had."

"Hmm."

"And although they had the summer camp, they did special things with us. We visited Luray Caverns and the thoroughbred farm next door. I used to love riding the horses there."

"The caverns and horses sound familiar. I can remember seeing the different stalactites and stalagmites."

"You used to love the caves."

"Probably the reason I'm a geology major."

"Maybe." She pointed out the truck window. "We had an entire play area over here, especially when we were too young to spend nights at the campground."

"I'm surprised we haven't seen your Colin rolling over here yet."

She couldn't hold back a smile at the mention of his name. "He's working with his horses today, but he called earlier, while you were sleeping."

"He could have hooked us up with some food. You starve a brother."

"If you had gotten out of bed, we would have stopped some place, but you wanted to sleep in.

Now you'll have to settle for a ham sandwich when we get to the camp."

"Travel a couple of thousand miles to help you and you starve me."

Noelle chuckled. "Free labor has to work to earn meals."

Gregory shook his head.

There was a lot of work to do that day, but Colin was coming by as soon as he could get away, and Noelle wanted to get as much done as possible before Greg left.

Slowly she exited the truck and stood in front of the old house, letting her memories warm her.

"I'm glad they left it to you," Greg said as he came up alongside her.

"Me, too."

He chuckled. "I didn't mean it like that."

She turned to him. "I guess I can see beyond the rough edges."

"Hell of an eyesight."

Noelle climbed the front steps, and using her key for the first time, she unlocked and opened the door. The place smelled of paint and age, and the rooms were cold, but she felt as if she'd stepped into heaven.

She walked through each room. A wide hallway

led to the back of the house and ended at the first-floor bathroom. To the right of the entrance was the dining room and in back of it was the kitchen. Surprisingly, the old fridge still ran. Noelle turned on the water in the deep sink. It came through strong and clear.

Through the kitchen window, she saw a pile of wood out back just waiting for the fire. Her dad had told her he'd ordered it for her in case the electricity went off.

She walked into the living room on the left, with its huge river-rock fireplace. Then on into the bedroom her grandparents had used all of their married life.

Noelle climbed the stairs to the second floor. Two sizable bedrooms flanked the hall, with the bathroom between them. The upstairs foyer was the size of a regular room, with French doors that opened to the upstairs porch.

She'd make that area a sitting room. Already she could picture a couch and couple of chairs and bookcases. Comfortable for reading and gazing out the French doors.

The ceilings had been painted antique white, but the walls were washed, patched and primed, waiting for Greg and her to paint them.

The house was old, but the beautiful stained woodwork was in surprisingly good repair.

Greg shook his head as he came upstairs. "I have a whole week of winter break left. I can drive you back to Memphis or to Monterey. The folks won't mind if you stay with them until you decide what you want to do. As a matter of fact, Mom would love for you to come home."

Obviously, Greg didn't see the potential she saw in the house. She turned to him and spread her arms wide. "Now why would I want to leave all this?"

"Let's see if I can list the reasons. You're in the middle of nowhere. Alone. The outside looks terrible." He wrinkled his nose. "So does the inside."

Noelle tilted her chin. "A fresh coat of paint, curtains and my furniture will have this place looking like home before you leave."

Greg shook his head. "If you say so."

She looked through the windows facing the campground. In the distance a few more weathered buildings could be seen through the bare trees. She was sure their state of disrepair was worse than that of the house, since her parents had at least periodically made minimal repairs to the house. She hoped she could hire someone reasonable to make the campground repairs.

In the meantime, there was work to be done. "I have cleaning supplies in the trunk."

Her brother sighed. "You know love doesn't fix everything."

Noelle hit him and he chased her to the car.

It didn't take long to clean the inside since her father had done most of the work. At nine they drove to the nearest paint store for supplies. After getting some fast food, they returned and started painting. They worked on the upstairs bedrooms first since they hoped to sleep in them that night. Afterward they left the windows open to get rid of the sharp paint smell.

"This stuff is supposed to dry quickly. Hope it lives up to its label," Greg said.

"So do I," Noelle agreed.

By five they had completed the upstairs. They took a minute to survey their labor.

It was just as she'd said. After a long sleep, the house was awakening.

Colin had tried to get away all day. But so much work had backed up it seemed he'd been running since he set foot on the farm. And although he'd told Leila to expect guests for dinner, he'd failed to invite Noelle and Greg. He changed from his boots to his shoes and changed his pants and shirt before he drove to Noelle's. He had horse all over him. He badly needed a shower, but it would have to wait until he returned home.

When Colin drove into the yard Noelle and Greg were taking a mattress out of the truck. He pulled to a stop and hopped out.

"I'll take your end, Noelle," he said setting words to action.

"That's going upstairs."

"Hi," he said and kissed her lightly on the lips just before he moved away with the mattress. She had tied a bandana on her head, her luscious hair hidden beneath. She was splattered with paint.

"Man, you're going to regret offering to help," Greg said. "She's going to use you until she wrings you dry."

"She's been working you pretty hard, huh?"

"Yeah. And starving me, too."

"I have a remedy for that. I'm here to invite the two of you to dinner. Actually the invitation is from George."

"Yeah!" Gregory yelled and almost pumped the air before he remembered he was carrying a load.

"I'm not that bad," Noelle said. "I fed you."

"Barely." The men climbed the stairs and placed the mattress on the box spring and frame.

"I'll help Greg bring in the furniture. You just tell us where you want it to go," Colin said.

In between directing the men, Noelle put linens on the bed and towels in the bathroom.

"Thanks for the help," she said when they had finished.

"Think you'll be finished with the downstairs tomorrow?"

"Hope so."

"Then I'll try to make it here around the same time to help Greg." He turned to leave, then remembered a detail. "Dinner's at seven."

"Good," Noelle said. "Gives Greg time to hang the curtain rods before we leave."

Gregory groaned.

Noelle walked Colin to the door. His hand gently brushed across her cheek just seconds before his mouth touched hers. He battled conflicting emotions. One part of him wanted to take it slower—the part that told him he wasn't ready for heavy and serious—another part wanted to hold her tightly and never let go. She had connections to George and he respected the older man, but slowly he savored her taste, trying to satisfy his endless need.

Her shiver flowed from her body to his. He tightened his arms around her. He couldn't stop a heated moan from escaping. "I've wanted you in my arms all day."

"I missed you," she said, intense desire brightening her eyes. She inhaled and whispered his name. "You smell like horse."

"Better get used to it. I won't smell like horse tonight, though," he said stroking her back. "You got a lot of work done today."

She leaned back, putting a little distance between them. "Dad did most of it when he came. I wanted to see the campground today, but it's dark already."

"Getting you settled in is more important."

"True."

"Well, if you're going to make it to dinner on time, I have to leave," he said, but he didn't move. He drew her closer and kissed her once again.

Noelle was like a drug infusing his veins. His feelings for her frightened him in their intensity. Any other time he'd back off, not willing to lay his heart on the line, but with Noelle, he didn't have a choice. She stole his reason, his very sanity.

Reluctantly he pulled back and took in the luminous sheen of her eyes. "See you soon." He forced himself to leave, or they'd miss dinner completely.

Noelle watched Colin's truck drive away, the last ray of light catching the River Oaks Thoroughbred Farm logo on the side. She closed the door against the cold and leaned against it as she tried to control her desire. This was moving much too fast.

"Hey," Greg called down. "You going to get into that shower or what? I'm starving."

Noelle went upstairs where she found her brother hanging the curtain rods in her bedroom.

"I'll be finished here by the time you're out of the bathroom," he told her.

"I'm so dirty, a hot shower sounds like heaven." She wasted no more time. As the water washed away the grime from her body, so, too, did the desire clear from her mind. In its place were nerves as she realized the moment she'd been waiting for was finally here.

She was finally going to meet her grandfather.

Colin took his shower and decided to look in on Maggie Girl while he waited for Noelle. But as he was leaving, his father drove into the yard. Just his luck. He should have known his old man would come by to see the new mare. Not that his old man was interested in the horse.

Leander Mayes exited his Escalade and walked with Colin to Maggie Girl's stall. Colin took a carrot from a bucket and fed it to her.

"If this stud of yours is pulling in the money you want, I don't understand why it's necessary to buy the mare," his father said. "You already have racehorses out there."

"If we don't build on what we have, we'll end up the way we were when Grandpa bought in. Diamond Spirit is pulling in good money for the first time. His offspring are winning races and some are already producing their own offspring who are winning. He's one of the most sought-after thoroughbred sires." Although Colin felt the necessity to explain everything to his father, he knew the older man didn't get it. His interest wasn't in thoroughbreds. Leander had fought his father bitterly about buying into the farm. It was a huge bone of contention between Leander and Colin. But Colin wasn't going to give his father a reason to sell.

"We have company coming," he said, changing the subject. "Can you stay to dinner?"

"I'll stay," his father replied. "I want to spend some time with George. How is he?"

"The same."

Candice Poarch

George's nephew, William, was just getting out of his car. Colin always thought of him as Slick Willie.

When William saw Colin's dad, he came wearing a smile. "How are you, Leander? Good to see you."

"William."

"Just came to see how the old man was doing. Got to keep an eye on him."

More like on his money, Colin thought. William couldn't care two cents about George, but now that Mackenzie was gone, he hoped to become his uncle's main beneficiary.

Colin shook his head. As much as Colin wanted to see Noelle, the evening seemed to be doomed by the very people he didn't want to see.

Noelle didn't know what she had expected from George Avery, but not the impressive stone-and-wooden house. When she knocked, an older woman answered the door.

"You must be little Noelle," she said. "How you've grown. You don't remember me, do you?"

"I'm sorry."

"I'm Leila. Mackenzie used to bring you here when he gave you riding lessons. I used to make you clam chowder. He insisted on it because it was your favorite."

"It still is." Noelle tried to contain the dip in her stomach. "Have you met my brother?"

"Yes, I have. Mackenzie used to ride you both on his horse. You were too young to train."

Greg extended a hand. "It's a pleasure to meet you, ma'am."

"Manners, too. What a nice young man you are," she said. "They're all gathered in the sitting room." She lowered her voice to a whisper. "Unexpected guests. I had to stretch out dinner. But don't worry, Gregory, I made plenty for you. You're a growing boy."

Greg chuckled. "I appreciate that."

Noelle tried to contain her apprehension as she was led to the back of the house. There were three older men, but the oldest must be George Avery. She could only stare speechless. He had gray hair and from his baggy clothes she figured he'd recently lost weight. He was a handsome man. The few pictures she'd seen didn't do him justice. But there was a dullness to his eyes. The laugh lines around his mouth suggested he was prone to laughter, although there was a sternness to him now.

Greg had to nudge her side before she extended

a hand to Colin's father and then George's nephew before she shook the older man's hand.

"Welcome to River Oaks," George said. "I knew your grandparents well. They were wonderful people."

"Thank you."

"The children's camp had changed hands over the years. I think it was a cheerleader camp for a while until four years ago. My son went to the camp when your grandparents owned it. He looked forward to it each summer."

Noelle saw a photo on the table and nodded toward it. "Is that your son?"

"Yes." There was a catch in his voice.

Her legs felt like lead as she walked across the floor to see a photo of Mackenzie for the first time. There had been plenty of grainy pictures of her grandfather in old newspapers, but Mackenzie had kept a low profile. She picked up the framed photo. Clearly he favored his father.

Colin came up beside her and handed her a champagne flute. She carefully placed the photo back on the table and took the glass from him.

"Congratulations on your first day home," he said, clinking his glass to hers. After a sip he slid an arm around her waist. "I'm glad you're here."

"Me, too." She was thinking she had feelings for this man that she'd never envisioned. Maybe this could grow into a meaningful relationship, after all. She'd expected him to be ready to move on, especially now that he was home, where she was sure he had his pick of women.

Finally she was in her grandfather's home. She'd wanted this so long she had difficulty wrapping her mind around the fact that she was here. She was so nervous that she was sure she was going to make a huge social blunder, like spilling the champagne on his beautiful wood floors.

Leila called them to dinner half an hour later. Colin and George sat at each end of a table that could comfortably seat fourteen. The antique furniture was heavy and the wallpaper and curtains were elegant.

"I keep trying to get you to retire, Uncle George," William said. "It's time for you to cut back and enjoy yourself."

Colin tensed.

"You don't retire from the thoroughbred business," George said.

"It's too much for you. Mama was just saying she wished she saw more of you. This job is 24/7. It hardly gives you time to enjoy your family."

"Your mother is free to visit me whenever she pleases. We have plenty of room and we won't trip over each other. Just as long as she stays out of Leila's way." George sighed, obviously thinking of his son. "My whole life is here. My wife and I lived our entire marriage here. My son lived here before he married, and he came back after the divorce. I don't want to be anywhere else."

How selfish of William to suggest George give up the only thing that gives him pleasure, Noelle thought.

"Still, you could make a nice little profit off this place."

"You're right there," Leander Mayes said.

George shook his head. "Colin and I are doing very well for the first time in a long time. Diamond Spirit's continuing to bring in money as a sire. And several of our other horses have been in the money on the track."

William was unconvinced. "Then this is the time to sell, when you can make top dollar."

"Once again," Leander agreed.

"I'm not selling, William. So let's enjoy our company without a business discussion." George changed his focus to Noelle. "What shape is the camp in?" he asked.

"I haven't had the opportunity to look at it yet, but Dad says it needs some work. I've moved into the house and I'm trying to get it in shape while Greg's here. Next week I'll tackle the camp."

"If you need help with selecting carpenters and contractors, I know the good ones. I'll be happy to help you."

"Thank you. I'm sure some repairs are in order."

Noelle was watching Colin. She knew what this business meant to him and what a strain it must be having people in his family against it. She stretched out her foot and caressed his leg. His piercing gaze met hers. His expression quickly changed from frustration to arousal.

Colin followed Noelle home. "Finally I have you to myself," he said.

"Why is William trying to convince Mr. Avery to sell his farm?"

"The greedy bastard wants George to leave everything to him."

"Oh."

"Yeah. He doesn't care about George. Doesn't spend time with him to help him get over his grief. Doesn't make suggestions. Just wants him to sell the farm at a good profit and leave him a bundle when he dies. He knows the farm is valuable. We're cash-poor, but the assets are worth a fortune." Colin shook his head. "You wouldn't believe the people coming out of the woodwork now that the farm is prospering. Right after Mackenzie died, some woman he dated claimed he had a child by her in college. Can you believe her? Said he owed her back child support."

"What happened?"

"George's lawyer handled it. They could use George to test the DNA. When his lawyer told her they'd be willing to accept the girl, but first they had to DNA-test her, she backed off. Said maybe she was mistaken. You can't believe what that did to him. People are so thoughtless."

Noelle's stomach roiled with tension. Why *would* someone lie like that? she wondered as they entered the house and headed upstairs to the little foyer where she'd put the couch and bookshelves.

Noelle took Colin's coat and put it on her bed.

"It's cozy up here," he said.

"I like it."

Greg had already disappeared into his room and closed the door. He was probably fast asleep by now. He'd worked pretty hard today.

"Another early day tomorrow?" Noelle asked.

Colin nodded. "I can't stay long, but I just wanted a few minutes alone with you."

"And maybe you should rescue George from his nephew."

"He's gone already. He never stays long. Just long enough for George to remember to make him the main beneficiary."

"How sad. George has another sister, doesn't he?"

Colin nodded. "She's a nice lady. She visits sometimes. Spends a few days. She's trying to get him to visit her, but he doesn't like to be away from the farm." In frustration, he leaned forward and scrubbed a hand over his face. "I wish I could help him. Mackenzie meant the world to him. I know he's been dealt a low blow. And it's going to take some time to get over it. But I feel so...incapable."

Noelle heard the agony in his voice and wished she could ease it. She rubbed his back.

"I think you being there helps. It's going to take time for him to recover," she said and felt sad because she couldn't reveal who she was, not after someone had already tried to cheat George.

Colin nodded and stood. "I have to go. I'll try to make it by to help Greg with the furniture tomorrow evening. It might be after dark before I get here."

"That's fine, thanks." Noelle wanted to tell him

they could handle it alone, but some of the furniture was pretty heavy, especially the sofa and armoire.

She walked him to the door where he captured her in his arms and kissed her. He held her as if he was reluctant to let her go.

When he finally did, cold air brushed over Noelle. She quickly closed the door behind him and shivered. Rubbing her arms, she went upstairs where she changed into sweats and got into bed. Sleep proved elusive. She couldn't stop thinking of George Avery. What a fix. To have the one person who truly loved you gone. And the ones left were circling like vultures for what they could get.

Suddenly Noelle felt sad for the kindly man. She understood why Colin was fond of him. A man of quiet dignity, George was the perfect cultured Southern host. He'd gently put William in his place without breaking stride and had then changed the conversation. He got his point across without indignation and without raising his voice.

Her grandfather was hurting. Noelle hated to see anyone in pain. Would it help if he knew he had a granddaughter? How would her father feel if she became involved with him? Mackenzie was dead so he wasn't a threat to Franklin. She and her father had never talked about it, although he knew she was here to see her grandfather. He accepted it and didn't seem to be intimidated by it. Or at least he pretended he wasn't. Noelle closed her eyes briefly. She loved her father. Couldn't ask for a better one. And she didn't understand her need to know the man who'd donated sperm for her.

Noelle sighed. She couldn't reveal her identity. Colin would think she came to Virginia for the same reason William visited the older man or for the reason that woman had pretended Mackenzie fathered her child—for what they could get. Colin had a great deal of influence over George. He'd think she, too, was there for monetary reasons.

No, she couldn't reveal her identity. But maybe she could become more involved with George. Maybe she could volunteer to take him to grief-counseling sessions or something. Then maybe Colin would see her intentions were genuine.

Why did it matter so much? she asked herself.

Because Colin mattered.

Noelle sighed. She was finally getting sleepy, but she was saddened.

Never in a million years would she have thought she and Colin would date. Not the womanizer. But he seemed to have changed.

Could a man really change that much?

Chapter 5

"Noelle." Colin's deep husky tone was a gentle balm early the next morning. He sounded as if he'd been up for hours. Noelle moaned and rolled over. She snuggled up tightly beneath the covers.

"How can you be so energized this early in the morning?" she asked, the phone tucked close against her ear.

"I'm sipping my second cup of coffee and I'm watching the the mountains against the moonlight," he said. The timbre of his voice decreased. "It's the best I can do since I don't have you in my arms."

Noelle had been filled with contentment until his

statement hit her. He threw her immediately into a sensual haze, wondering what kind of lover he'd be. He was definitely a morning person who'd wake her slowly with his kisses. Her skin felt hot beneath the blankets and she peeled one of them back.

They talked for nearly five minutes while his words stroked her slowly and sweetly. Finally they said goodbye and she hung up the phone.

Noelle wasn't a morning person. Usually she made it up at seven, not five-thirty, but she had a lot to do. The first order of business was a fresh pot of coffee for energy. She dressed, woke Gregory up and went downstairs. They should have at least brought in a table and chairs, she thought as she took meager supplies out of the fridge—just bacon, eggs and a loaf of bread. She needed to make a trip to town to purchase food.

By the time she cooked breakfast and carried it upstairs to the sitting area, Greg had dressed. He came out of the bathroom looking sleepy. She handed him coffee. "A cup of joè should get you moving."

"I need to get back to school so I can get some rest," he said.

"You're still young and strapping. You can handle it."

After breakfast they painted downstairs. By noon, they had finished the living room and dining room. Then they changed clothes and went into town for groceries, stopping first for lunch at Salamanders. After they selected items from the display cases, they took a seat in the dining area.

"Dad called last night," Noelle said. "He forgot about the time change. You were fast asleep."

"Yeah. I was asleep before my head hit the bed. I woke up in my clothes this morning. Wow!" he said looking behind her. "If only she was a little younger."

Noelle followed his interested gaze until it lit on a woman at a table behind them. She looked familiar, but Noelle couldn't place her. She had a pretty round face with a dark-brown complexion and dimpled cheeks. She took off her hat and ran her hand across her short black, naturally curly hair. Noelle frowned. She remembered those dimples, but couldn't place them. Not wanting to be caught staring, she faced her brother.

"I think we'll paint the kitchen and the bathroom tonight and leave the downstairs bedroom for tomorrow morning," Noelle said.

"What are you going to do with the bedroom? Make it into a family room?"

"No. I don't need a formal living room, so that room will be the family room and entertainment area. I'm turning the downstairs bedroom into an office."

Greg groaned. "Which means I'm back to sleeping on the couch when we all visit."

"The office is large enough for a sleep sofa. So you'll have someplace to sleep."

"I hope you get cable. The reception is terrible here."

"You're full of complaints, aren't you? I'll have satellite when you return, just to please you."

"Noelle?" a voice called out. "Are you Noelle Greenwood?"

Noelle focused on the woman Greg had commented on earlier.

"Yes, I am."

"Oh, my gosh. I'm Casey. Cassandra Reed."

"I can't believe it. I thought you looked familiar. I haven't seen you since…"

"Summer camp. How I enjoyed those summers."

"So did I. This is my brother, Gregory."

"Pleasure to meet you," he said.

"Same here. I saw your grandparents a lot just before they died."

"Actually," Noelle said, "I'm opening the

summer camp again. I've moved into my grandparents' house and I'll be getting the camp in shape over the next few months."

"Aren't you lucky! I'm sharing a three-bedroom house with two other women. Real estate here is expensive. I'm saving up for a place of my own. So when are you opening the camp?"

"This summer," Noelle said. "It will focus on computer and investment skills."

"Wow! You need to start advertising. I have nephews and nieces my sisters want to get rid of for a few weeks."

Noelle laughed. "I hope our parents didn't feel that way about us."

"I'm teasing. I dote on them. But my sisters and brothers attended that camp, too. It was such a good experience that I'm sure they would want their children to have it, as well."

"I should have brochures ready by the middle of next month," Noelle assured her.

"In the meantime, I'll let them know. We have to get together soon." She dug in her purse and gave Noelle a card. "My address and phone numbers."

"Here's my cell number. They haven't hooked up the landline yet." Noelle tore a piece of paper from a pad in her purse.

"I have to get back to work," Casey said. "My boss is nice, but he's strict about lunch hours. Nice meeting you, Gregory."

"Same here." He watched her until she went out the door.

"Sit down and finish your food, brother."

"She's a babe. And the way those jeans fit her... But I guess she's as old as you."

"She's a year or two younger," Noelle said.

"Oh. I'm just a couple of years younger than you."

"You're a kid in comparison."

"I think I like older women."

Noelle rolled her eyes heavenward. "Give me a break," she said, just before she saw Colin strolling toward her.

"Hi. Thought I saw your car out there." He bent and kissed her. His lips were cold.

"What're you doing in town?"

"On my way from the training track," he said, pulling out the chair beside her and sitting down. They were so close his arm brushed hers, sending sparks of awareness through her. "Was that Casey I saw leaving?" He took a sip of her hot chocolate.

"Yes. We went to camp together." Suddenly the food churned in Noelle's stomach and she lost her appetite. Had Colin and Casey dated?

She had no time to ponder that because Colin asked, "So what did y'all get done this morning?"

"Just the living and dining rooms. We'll get to the kitchen this afternoon."

"Coming right along," he said.

She nodded. "I need to start looking for someone to make repairs on the campground. I haven't had the time to go there yet."

"George recommended Carp. But I have to tell you up front that he's been having some problems since his wife left him. Hasn't been too reliable. But he needs someone to give him a chance. He'll work cheaper than the regular construction firms if you'll give him a chance to prove himself. If you're afraid of taking a chance, he'll recommend someone else."

"Does he do good work?"

"Great work. A regular contractor would cost you a fortune, but the work won't be any better. He's done a lot of work for us at the farm."

"I'll try him."

"Good. I'll bring him by tomorrow. Unfortunately, I have to go now." He stood, then leaned down to kiss her.

Noelle felt her body heat up, burning to ashes whatever anxiety she'd had. She watched him until he left the building.

"Earth to Noelle." Greg shook his head. "I never thought my never-take-a-man-seriously sister would fall for a guy so fast."

Noelle just sighed.

"I'm going to pick out something for dinner. There's nothing to eat at your house," he added.

"We're going to stop by the grocery store next and I'm cooking dinner tonight. You deserve one of my home-cooked meals."

The paint was barely dry by the time Colin came over and helped Gregory move in the kitchen and living-room furniture.

True to her word, Noelle prepared dinner and Colin stayed to eat with them. Afterward, Gregory escaped upstairs to watch a DVD on the television in Noelle's room. Colin made a fire in the living-room fireplace, and sat in front of it on the rug.

"Sorry I'm so grungy, but I didn't have time to change before I left," he said.

"I'm not Miss Pristine, either."

She looked good to him, Colin noted as he watched her backside when she leaned over to put cups of hot chocolate on the coffee table. She sat beside him and he pulled her close.

"My father said there was some good furniture

stored in the basement. I have to look down there to see if I can use anything. I'm hoping they have a desk."

"You might fix up that space one day to add to your living area."

"I doubt it. I don't need more room. Plus it's so dark and it needs rewiring. And the views from up here are breathtaking in every direction."

"I think I like that most about the farm." He was really thinking that *she* was breathtaking.

He should go home and get some sleep, but he couldn't force himself to leave. He just couldn't wrap his mind around how she'd thrown him for a loop or the fact that he wanted to spend every spare second with her. As much as he loved the thoroughbred business, she gave him added incentive to work even harder so he would be able to offer her something. Never had he considered the big *M* word before, but now all he could think of was having Noelle for himself. Of how he wanted to pay off the farm's debts and save something for their future. Every morning her face was the first one he wanted to see. And the last thing he wanted was for her to leave after summer camp to work someplace else for the rest of the year. He wanted her near him. God, he wanted her in his home.

But he couldn't make any promises yet. He'd wait and see how his life played out. First he'd have to get his father off his back about selling the farm. With that threat over his head, he couldn't begin to think about marriage. It hadn't mattered before. But now everything, his whole life, had changed in a couple of weeks.

The next afternoon Colin took some time off from the farm to hunt down Carp. He drove into the yard with the carpenter, who was one of the best in the area, that is, if you could get him sober enough to get the work done. He still did odd jobs at the farm, but someone always had to keep a close eye on him to make sure he didn't sneak a drink. They couldn't allow drunks around the horses.

Carp's father was a carpenter and he'd started working with his father when he was young. The older men would tease him about being a little carpenter and called him Carp. The nickname stuck and nobody called him by his real name, Benjamin.

"Can't believe Epps's granddaughter is back," Carp said. "Thought the daughter would eventually sell that place." He shook his head. "That good land going to waste. What a shame."

"At least it's going to be put to good use now," Colin said, dodging a pothole.

"Been so long, place couldn't be in any kind of shape. Don't keep up a building, it goes to seed."

"Except Epps built sturdy buildings. I think it held up pretty well."

Carp grunted.

"I'm counting on you getting those buildings in shape. It's January. You have until June. I could repair them in that length of time."

"Why is it so important to you?"

Colin darted a glance at the older man. "You dipping in my business, Carp?"

Carp grinned. "Yeah."

Colin chuckled. "You just make sure she doesn't decide to move back to Memphis to that computer job. I want her right here."

"Just drop me off at the campsite. I'll look things over while you find her. You can take your time. It'll take a while to go through everything."

Colin drove the rutted road to the campsite. As soon as Carp got out he headed for Noelle's place. The yard needed serious work; the plants her grandparents had put in had grown wild over the years. Dormant now, they'd need trimming come spring.

Colin stopped beside the rental truck and loped

up the stairs to knock on the door. Noelle opened it wearing a bandana, old jeans and an oversize sweatshirt. Even with paint splatters as her only makeup, and with all her curves hidden, desire still hit him hard. He had it bad.

Colin pulled her into his arms and kissed her until he got his fill.

"Hi," he said when he came up for air.

"Hi, yourself," she said, laughing.

"I think I taste paint."

"You taste like coffee. Yum. Come on in out of the cold," she said. His arm was still around her waist. "We've painted the last room, thank God. And I took a quick trip to the basement. There's a nice desk down there and a couple of chairs and a dining-room table I want to bring up here."

"Greg and I'll do it later on this evening. Leila thinks you need fattening up. Said your grandmother would be scandalized."

"Oh? And what do you think?"

He didn't need an excuse to let his eyes roam over her. "I told her you're perfect the way you are."

Heat infused Noelle's face.

"She sent coffee, with coffee cake and a whole plastic container of clam chowder. You made quite an impression on her. She liked your grandparents.

She likes you, too. Thinks you're just the woman to get me to settle down. What do you think?"

"I think it was kind of her to send food and I can't wait to dig into the chowder. I have to thank her."

"Coward." They both knew she was evading the reference to his settling down, but he let the subject ride for now. "She has an ulterior motive. She wants to enroll her grandchildren in the camp."

"We have room. How many grandchildren?"

"Three that are the right age."

"I'll make sure there's room for them."

"Carp is outside looking over the buildings," he said.

"You sobered him up?"

"I caught him on a good day. After he gets one of the cabins in decent shape you might want to let him stay there out of the way of temptation until he finishes."

"I don't have a problem with that."

"Where's Greg?"

"He ran to town to get a new DVD. He was tired of being cooped up in the house."

"Wish I could stay, but you might want to go down to the campsite in an hour or two, after Carp has a chance to go through the buildings. And don't lift any furniture. I'll help Greg."

"I'm not helpless, you know."

"Yeah, well, we'll save that back for other things."

Noelle blushed again. She knew he was teasing her, but she couldn't help wondering what the real thing would be like.

An hour later Noelle grabbed her coat and knit hat, and hurried to the car to drive the short distance to the camp, where she found Carp in the kitchen.

The radio had predicted snow by morning. Already, thick clouds covered the sky, giving the camp an even more dilapidated look.

There were three huge buildings. The girls' and the boys' dorms were on either side of the dining and entertainment hall, which was closer to the lake. A few smaller cabins, mainly for the workers, were farther away. Noelle went to the girls' dorm first, but the door was locked. The cafeteria was also locked. She went to the last building, the boys' dorm, and found that door unlocked.

"Hello?"

"Back here," a voice called out.

Noelle followed the voice and ended up in the bathroom. The dorms were on two levels with several rooms on each floor. Each room slept eight.

There was a communal bath on each floor with six shower stalls and eight commodes.

A man of about forty came out of the shower area.

"I'm Noelle Greenwood," she said, extending her hand.

The man held his hands up. "I'm too grimy. Benjamin Gaines, but everyone calls me Carp."

"Pleased to meet you. So, how does it look?"

"Better than I expected. A few boards need to be replaced in the dining hall and part of the roof. Something must have fallen on it."

While Noelle fought a shiver from the cold temperature, beads of sweat had gathered on Carp's forehead. A strong forehead with lines of concentration. The planes of his face appeared as harsh as if he'd lived a hundred years.

"Most of the work will be minor. It's going to need a lot of landscaping, though. You're going to need to hire someone full-time from spring until late summer to handle it anyway. I know someone who won't charge you a fortune. He's retired, but he works with kids who need summer jobs. Don't worry about your kids because he keeps a strict eye on them."

"All right."

"I used to come here during the summers when I was a kid. My parents couldn't afford to pay the full price, but your grandparents gave my folks a discount. They even gave me the camp clothes so no one ever knew I couldn't afford to be here. I'm just grateful I'm getting a chance to pay them back. I'll do a good job for you and I'm not going to charge you an arm and a leg. I won't fix things that don't need fixing just to make more money. I'm going to save anywhere I can."

"Thanks, Carp. I really appreciate it."

They moved from the bathroom to one of the bedrooms. The room was an empty shell.

"I hope I don't have to buy all new beds," she said.

"I found some in a shed. You'll probably need new mattresses. But you can probably buy them in bulk."

Noelle glanced out the window. She had a good view of the camp. It resembled a ghost town. Deserted. The bare trees and rolling mountains behind it made it seem isolated. She looked past the broken windows and weather-roughened buildings and imagined smiling children horseback-riding, swimming in the lake, swinging on old tires, sitting at computers while she taught them something new and exciting.

"Your grandparents had the gift of love and excelled at making people believe they were

Candice Poarch

special," Carp said. "Deep in my gut I know you'll make this place as successful as they did."

"I hope so," she said. She had been apprehensive when Colin had first suggested Carp, but now she was glad he'd chosen him. The man had a history here. He'd liked her grandparents. This had been a special place for him. He'd help her return this place to its former glory.

"Hey, George, could you take a look at Ranger's leg? Looks a little swollen." Colin had grabbed a sandwich from the kitchen and was eating it on his way back to the barn when he spotted George gazing out the window. If somebody didn't intervene, he'd be there for hours.

"The trainer can handle it," George said.

"I know, but he could use a second opinion."

It was true. The trainer could handle it, but Colin wanted to get George more involved in something. He spent most of his time moping around. And that wasn't like him at all. Instead of getting back into the swing of things, it seemed the older man was sinking deeper into depression.

"Nah. You go ahead."

"What're you doing?" Colin asked.

George shook his head.

"Did you go over the payroll?"

"Not yet."

"Can you take care of that for me?" Colin asked. "I'm running a little behind."

George shrugged. "Yeah, sure. I'll get to it."

"So, what do you think of Noelle?" Colin came to stand beside George while he munched on his sandwich.

"Hmm?"

"Noelle. What did you think of her?"

"Reminds me of her grandmother. Seems nice. Good to have the camp opened again. Mackenzie used to work there, you know. Part-time some summers when he was in college. I never understood it. He had enough work to do around here. But he liked teaching the kids. Especially Noelle. I remembered when he taught her to ride. She was afraid of the horses at first. She wasn't accustomed to being around them in California. Mackenzie thought since her family was from here, she should know. He was really patient. They would ride for hours. For some reason, he was taken by that girl." George shook his head. "Don't know why he took such a liking to her. And she followed him around like a little puppy." George sighed. "Her grandparents were my very good friends, as close as your grandfather. Seems like everybody's dying off. I just wish Mackenzie'd had children. He was good with them. Wonder why they never..." George sighed again. "I'll work on the paperwork later."

"Okay, George. Why don't you have some lunch?" The older man had lost so much weight in the last few months, he was melting away. "George?"

"Yeah?"

"Have you given thought to maybe attending a grief-support group or seeing someone who could, you know, help you get through this?"

He continued to gaze out the window. "Will it bring Mackenzie back?"

"No, but—"

"Then I'm not wasting my time."

"It could make the pain more bearable."

He offered a sad smile. "Nothing can do that, son. All my friends are gone. And now my son. It's just..." He walked off.

Colin didn't realize Leila had witnessed the exchange until he heard her sniffle. She wiped the tears from her eyes with her apron.

"Lord, that poor man has suffered so," she said.

"I don't know what to do, Ms. Leila. I wish I could do something, anything."

"Nothing you can do, child. Time will heal."

"It's like he's given up on life. I have to help him find a reason to go on. And the farm isn't enough any longer."

"Lord, child, we work our fingers to the bone to make things better for our children."

"Even though Dr. Mackenzie didn't work at the farm."

"In a sense he did. As a vet, he loved to care for animals. If he'd had children, one of them might have taken after George." She dabbed at her eyes and sighed. "Well, it's too late for that now. He was right about that gal. Dr. Mackenzie doted on her. Of all the children at the camp, she was the one he spent most of his time with. Used to let her stay in his office when she was a little one, talk to her about the animals. He was so patient with her. As patient as he was with his animals." She blew her nose in the tissue. "Lord knows, he was something with those animals. And they knew he was special. It was like he reserved all his patience for them. Did you give her the food?"

"Yes, I did, and she sends her thanks."

"She always liked clam chowder, even when she was a little thing. And that brother of hers is at an age that he'll eat enough for four people."

Colin chuckled.

"I can't stay wasting my day with you," she said, turning toward the kitchen. "I've got a million things to do."

"Keep an eye on the old man, will you?" Colin headed to the door.

"I always do," Leila said as he went out the back door. Colin followed her out. It felt like snow. He tugged his gloves on and pulled his collar up as he headed to the truck.

"Do you know what this room is missing?" Noelle asked.

"Curtains?" Greg offered.

"No. An island. Like the one in Mom's kitchen, but smaller."

"Speaking of Mom, she called while you were inspecting the camp, just to see how we were. I made sure to tell her we got a week's worth of work done in one day."

"I'm sure she believed you."

"She believes everything I say, just like you're Dad's angel."

"You keep believing that." He was partially right, though.

"Umm. This is the best clam chowder I've ever tasted," Greg said.

"All food is delicious to you."

"Hey, you're working me half to death, and with a pauper's wages."

"You're eating your wages."

Greg shook his head and spooned up more soup. "Is Colin coming over tonight?"

"I doubt it. But I think I'll ride Maggie Girl tomorrow if he lets me. She must miss me by now. Be nice for her to see a familiar face."

"Until now, I would never believe you were going to do it."

"Open the camp?"

He nodded and patted her shoulder. "I'm happy for you. And you've even got me interested in my cave now. I'll be back over spring break to check it out."

Chapter 6

In the next few days, Noelle got most of her boxes unpacked. Greg installed all the curtain rods and she hung most of the curtains she'd brought with her, and drove out to purchase some new ones.

The kitchen island stayed on her mind, so when Carp came to give her the estimate for repairs on the campground, she asked him if he could install one. "I need a space for a dishwasher, too," she told him.

Carp thought a minute, then said, "I have an island that someone had me build then decided against it. The woman couldn't make up her mind about what she wanted." He walked to the right of the sink and opened the cabinet doors. "I can build a space here for the dishwasher." He glanced around the kitchen. "One thing's for sure. You've got plenty of storage here with all the cabinets. But I know how women are. There's never enough storage."

The cabinets in the kitchen covered three walls. Her grandmother had kept them in good condition and, she realized thankfully, the renters over the years had also. There were a couple of worn spots, but for the most part they were pretty, with scalloped edges on the section above the windows.

"I could install the island where the table is now. There's even a ledge and you can put a couple of chairs underneath if you want to eat there. You can place your pots and pans in it or I could build you a ceiling rack to hang them on."

"Oh, I've always wanted that. Could you really?"

"Sure. Ceiling's high enough. I'll get on it right away. I'll include it in the price of the island." He took a tape measure out and recorded the length and depth of the kitchen on a pad from his pocket. Then he tested the ceiling for a beam where he could nail things.

"I've got nothing to do the rest of the day if you want to come over to my place to see the island," he told her. He jotted the directions then he left.

Noelle didn't hold much hope that the island would be very good since he'd said the woman had turned it down, but Carp seemed rather proud of it and the estimate was reasonable.

"Well, I guess we better take a look," she said to Greg later.

"You don't sound too optimistic."

"I'm not, but what will it hurt? Carp looked as if he hadn't taken a drink in a while. Maybe this job is giving him a new lease on life."

Carp lived twenty minutes away, in a stone ranch house with a detached two-car garage.

"It's right in here," he said, opening the garage door onto a complete workshop. Carp went to the corner where something was covered with a huge cloth. Gingerly, he peeled the cloth off.

"Oh, my gosh. This is beautiful," Noelle said when she saw the island. The stained wood shone, as did the granite top. She walked around it, looking for flaws, but there were none. She opened the doors. There were movable shelves, making retrieving items easy.

Carp cleared his throat. "Since she's already paid for the materials, I won't charge what I would normally charge."

"Sold. Thank you." The woman must have been crazy.

"If it's okay with you, I'll deliver it this afternoon and build the rack for your pots. I've got everything I need right here."

Noelle couldn't wait. The camp and the house—and her future—were beginning to take shape.

Around five Colin called.

"What's that banging noise?" he asked.

Noelle went to the office and closed the door. Since the kitchen was across the hall, it only cut the noise a little. "Carp and a helper are installing ceiling hangers and an island in the kitchen. It's gorgeous. Wait until you see it."

"I'd rather see you."

"You always know the right thing to say, don't you?"

"I want to take you and your brother to dinner."

"I owe you, George and Leila dinner."

"Wait until you get settled in. Tonight is on me. Isn't your brother leaving soon?"

"In two days. I'm going to miss him. This week has gone by so quickly."

"I'll make sure you don't miss him when he's gone," Colin assured her.

"Is that a promise?"

* * *

Colin held Noelle's hand as they walked toward the restaurant. They'd chosen a cozy little place off Main Street. Noelle was something else. Any other woman would want him to take her to a five-star restaurant with all the fixings. Yet she'd chosen a comfortable place known to serve delicious food.

His relationship with Noelle felt new, different from anything he'd ever experienced. Although they'd known each other a very short time, it seemed they'd known each other for months. Usually he would have had her in bed by now, but she was special and he wanted to do this differently. He felt comfortable with her, as if, for once, he could be himself.

He felt pretty good right now. A few of their horses were coming in the money. Maybe not win, place or show at every race, but they were holding their own. And some of Diamond Spirit's offspring were winning. Things were finally looking up, he thought as he opened the door for Noelle.

They hadn't been there more than ten minutes after sitting down and ordering when a woman squealed, grabbed Colin and kissed him right on the mouth.

Noelle couldn't believe it. "I haven't seen you since before Christmas," the woman said, unwilling to let him go. "When are you coming by?"

Colin stood. "Hi, Simone. Meet Noelle and Gregory. They're new in town."

The woman barely threw them a glance before she questioned Colin again.

"I've been out of town," he replied. "And you know how busy it gets at the farm." He tried to untangle himself diplomatically, but the woman wasn't willing to relinquish her hold just yet, reminding Noelle of just whom she was dealing with. He probably had a woman around every corner.

"How's your father?" he asked.

"Doing well. I saw your brother the other week. He said he was coming out to visit soon. I've got a place out here now so I'll be closer to my parents. So when am I going to see you?"

"Brought a new mare. Keeping me pretty busy right now."

Only when the server brought their food did she leave. "Nice seeing you again," he said.

"Don't be a stranger, sugar. I enjoyed myself at the track with you the other day. We're going to have to do it again soon." She made sure to give him a hug before she left, leaving an imprint of her lipstick on his cheek.

Colin laughed and sat down, looking in every direction except directly at Noelle. "At least the service is quick," he said, rubbing his hands together.

"Old friend?" Noelle asked through gritted teeth.

"She's a reporter and she's doing an article on the farm for her paper. We've known each other since we were children," he said. "River Oaks needs all the publicity it can get."

"Hmm."

"So, Greg, maybe you'll have time to tour the area when you visit again," Colin said. "I don't think you got to see much of the town this trip."

"No, but I'm coming back over spring break to check out my cave."

"Cave?"

"Yeah. My grandparents left me a cave with commercial possibilities. It's boarded up, but I think I'll take a look."

"Pretty neat. There are quite a few in the area."

"Yeah."

Noelle sighed inwardly. Colin was everything she wanted in a guy, except she wished he were more the one-woman kind of man. With his history, she knew she wasn't going to be able to hold on to him. She didn't want to be knocking into old girl-friends every time she turned around.

Maybe she was building herself up for a fall. The

smidgen of fear that was never far away roiled in her stomach. She was falling for him much too fast. And for the first time, she saw him as the rake that he was. Perhaps they should just be friends. They were next-door neighbors after all.

Even as the thought emerged, she knew it was already too late. She burned as hot for him as a match on a log doused with gasoline.

And now he sat all innocent, as if that woman's intrusion meant nothing. As far as Noelle knew, the woman was still waiting on the sidelines for him to renew their relationship. Maybe he left all his women like that. And maybe she was being paranoid. For the first time, Noelle felt weak, self-conscious. She'd never felt that way before and she hated the fact that she was questioning her own self-esteem.

She didn't want to come off as one of those suspicious women who was afraid to trust her man out of her sight, but she was running up against Colin's reputation. She glanced at him. The first thing she saw was the imprint of that woman's lips on his cheek. He'd left it there like a talisman.

"I'd like for you and Greg to spend tomorrow afternoon at my place," Colin told her, interrupting her thoughts. "Bring a swimsuit. There's an indoor pool and whirlpool. They built it so Granddad could exercise after he got arthritis. And we'll get to show Greg a little about a thoroughbred farm before he leaves."

"I'd like that," Greg said.

Noelle didn't respond.

Colin had never expected to run into one of his old dates. Simone was always a little too willing to please, a little too friendly. He glanced at Noelle. She was concentrating on eating. He wanted to gather her hand in his, but he was good at reading women and he wouldn't put it past her to stab him with her knife if he touched her. He started gathering his reasoning skills, because he knew that once he dropped them off and Greg disappeared, he was going before the firing squad.

"Maybe you should wipe the lipstick off," Noelle said.

"Oh." Laughing, he took the napkin and swiped at his lips and cheek. "Simone was always a little too friendly."

"I'm sure."

He had a lot of explaining to do, Colin thought. He hadn't given the kiss a second thought, but he knew Noelle had. Then he began to get ticked off. He hadn't lived the life of an angel, but he'd changed since meeting Noelle. Of course, what reason did she have to trust that? Maybe just because she *should* trust him.

"Okay, let's have it," Colin said when they were alone back at the house. "Simone is just a friend. Yes, we've dated, but it's over."

"If she's just a friend, what gives her the right to gather you up like a scarf?"

"I can't read women's minds."

"Humph. You know—"

"Look, you're the first woman I've felt something special for in years. I'm not about to screw around with someone when I have you."

"So what was this bit about the race track?"

"She's a reporter. I had to show her around. It's strictly business. She came one day and was hanging with one of my workers. She wanted to know about racing. Said she was doing an article on the farm and Diamond Spirit."

"That kiss wasn't strictly business."

"I know. And I didn't like that any more than you did. She can be a bit overwhelming."

"I bet."

"Come on, don't be like that. I dated her for a month. That's as far as it got. She was no more serious than I was. But I have to do what I can to promote the farm."

"And how far will you take it?"

"I do have integrity," he said, now angry. "I won't sell myself for it. What kind of man do you think I am?"

"I don't know. Quite frankly, you have a reputation and that leaves me a little uncertain about where we stand."

He tried to cut the irritation from his voice. "Look, you don't need to worry. I like you a lot. I'm not messing around on you. I won't screw this up."

"I'm counting on you being honest with me, Colin."

"I am. Come on. It's late. And I want you to enjoy the day with me tomorrow. I want to show you what I do."

She was annoyed and wasn't ready to forgive so easily. "You could have invited me earlier."

"I thought you needed to work on your place while Greg was here to help you, and you know that."

She had to concede he was correct there. But his connection with that other woman still bugged the heck out of her. Yet, what he said made sense. He ran a business. The woman was a reporter. He needed the publicity. And she knew George wasn't in any frame of mind to do it. It was his job.

"Okay," she conceded, "come on in and relax."

"I think I'll go so I can get up extra early and spend some time with you."

He moved closer and gathered her into his arms. "I need a little something to keep me going until I see you tomorrow."

She pursed her lips. "And what would that be?"

He pulled her tighter against him. "I can show you better than I can tell you." And then he kissed the tip of her ear tenderly, coaxingly, and moved his lips down her cheek. He nibbled her lips, not quite kissing her fully until anticipation almost had her melting into a puddle. Lord, this man could make her forget her own name, forget everything except him. When it seemed he'd never kiss her, his lips covered hers and his tongue swiped the seam of her lips, and then he was kissing her fully.

There was something about his scent, the way he held her, that appealed to her. But before she was completely satisfied, he pulled back as if he was reluctant to let her go. Those kisses left her churning with the ache of unexpected need.

"Don't forget the swimsuit," he said.

And then he was gone. Just like always.

She'd thought a man with his finesse could think of a hundred ways to get her alone to make love. Maybe he was making sure she was ready. She didn't know what his game was, but she'd been ready long ago. These little prim kisses and minutes of necking were getting old fast. Maybe *prim* was the wrong term. *Heated* was a better description.

Noelle climbed the stairs to her room once again. Alone.

The hardest thing Colin had ever done was walk away from Noelle. He wanted to carry her up those stairs and take her to bed. He wanted to love her until he was sated beyond wanting. He opened his truck door and sat, staring at her door, trying to cool the fire in his blood. Every muscle ached with tension.

The light in her room flicked on. In seconds he saw her silhouetted through the curtains. She was taking off her clothes.

Damn. Abruptly, he started the motor and lowered the window in the truck even though the temperature outside hovered around zero. He was burning up with desire and he needed to cool off. If it weren't for her brother, he'd be at her door that very minute. But Colin didn't want Noelle holding back. And she wasn't one of those women who could let loose and be free with lovemaking with her brother next door. Truth was, he didn't think he'd let her touch him with her brother that close.

Colin was still burning up. He unbuttoned his coat, but the short drive to his house failed to quench his desire.

He drove directly to the barn. His trainer was there wrapping a bandage around a horse's leg.

"What's wrong?" Colin asked.

"Leg's a little swollen." That wasn't unusual with racehorses. One had to be vigilant about taking care of impossibly thin legs that supported huge bodies. Wrapping it helped ease the swelling.

Colin laughed to himself. Too bad he couldn't ease his own swelling that way.

It was cold and misty when Noelle and Greg went to River Oaks. They drove up and down the rolling hills. They stopped at the guardhouse at the gate to show ID before they were allowed to enter the barn area.

"They have serious security here," Greg said.

"They have a prized horse. You wouldn't believe the security at some of these places."

Cresting a hill, Noelle got her first daylight view

from River Oaks property of the Blue Ridge Mountains. When they'd had dinner there, night had fallen by the time they'd arrived.

"It's something to look at, isn't it?" Greg asked.

"This is breathtaking," she said. "No wonder Colin wants to hold on to this place."

When she got her first view of Colin, he too was breathtaking, dressed in jeans and a jacket. When he saw her, he directed her where to park and then met her, kissing her lightly on the lips. Heat spread through her.

Noelle knew a little about the horse business from when she was a child and Mackenzie had brought her to the farm. But that had been years ago when her grandparents had still been alive.

"To get the true feel of a thoroughbred farm, you have to come early in the morning when a lot of activity is going on. That's when the horses get their workouts while the stables are cleaned." He smiled. "You might want to skip that part. Only horse lovers appreciate it."

A groom walked past with a chestnut. The horse nudged Colin on the shoulder. Without breaking a stride he pulled a carrot out of his pocket and fed it to the horse. The animal gulped it up quickly.

Colin patted him on the neck. "He loves carrots. He had a good workout this morning."

The groom tugged at the reins and got the horse moving.

Noelle saw a groom tuck carrots in his pocket from a bucket filled with them. One beside it was filled with apples.

"Your barn is impressive," she said. It was built of stone and stained wood.

"It was renovated a few years ago by Mennonite artisans. Each stall has an automatic heated waterer," Colin said.

It was midday feeding. "The horses are eating their individual mixture of oats, bran, vitamins and electrolytes," Colin said.

When she approached a stall with mare and foal, she wanted to stroke the foal. It was small and alert. The date of birth on the door showed it had been born just after the New Year. But it was suckling its mother while the mare ate her lunch.

"Takes your breath away, doesn't it?" Colin said. "I'm going to get you over here to see a birthing. You'll like that." But he wasn't watching the foal and mare; he was watching her.

Colin took her by the office where a woman was scheduling breeding sessions for Diamond Spirit and other stallions on the property. "We have to be very selective in choosing the mares we breed with Diamond Spirit," Colin said. "We want to breed only to established winning bloodlines or Diamond Spirit's offspring could be devalued."

The woman hung up the phone and Noelle finally saw her face.

"Casey, I didn't know you worked here," she said.

"I didn't know you knew the owner. I've been here a couple of years now. I love working with the horses. I have a nice view and a great boss."

"You're only saying that because I'm here," Colin muttered.

"You're right." She laughed. "But I'm serious. Unless he's in one of his moods, I couldn't ask for better."

"Casey shares a house with Simone and a local teacher," Colin said.

"Do you know Simone?" Casey asked Noelle.

"They met last night," Colin murmured.

"That explains why she came home throwing a hissy fit last night. Colin's name was mentioned along with 'some woman.' She doesn't take rejection very well."

Colin spread his arms wide. "Hey, she broke it off with me."

"Because you wouldn't settle down."

"I think on that note, we need to go inside and take a swim. Maybe eat snacks after. Got your suit?" he asked Noelle.

"I have it." She noticed Greg paying more attention to Casey.

"I'll be back in a couple of hours, Casey," Colin said, leading Noelle toward the door. But Greg stood where he was. "Greg, are you coming with us?"

He jumped. "What?"

"Come on," Noelle said. "We're interrupting Casey's work."

"No chance in your joining us, is there?" Greg asked Casey.

"I'm working," she said with a smile.

"Okay. I'll be back over spring break."

Casey outright chuckled. "I'll be here," she said indulgently. Noelle almost felt sorry for her brother, but she knew very well he'd be back checking out the ladies on campus in a few days.

"You won't settle, huh?" Noelle said.

"I wasn't ready then." He took her hand in his. "You know, I'm getting a bad rep here. I was younger then, and I hadn't found the woman to make me want to."

Noelle wouldn't mention it, but she wondered if he'd ever find the woman to make him settle down.

Noelle drove Greg to Dulles International Airport early the next morning.

"Thanks for all your help," she said.

"What are kid brothers for, if not free labor?"

"Okay, I owe you my first child."

"No, thanks. You're the one who likes the brats, not me."

She felt a tug in her gut. "I'm going to miss you."

"Don't get teary-eyed on me now. I'll be back before you have a chance to miss me."

He grabbed his bag from the backseat.

"Have fun at school," she called out.

He raised a hand and loped to the door.

Noelle watched him enter the terminal and drove off just before an officer came to urge her to move on. At least she was driving home against rush-hour traffic. Driving in had been stop and go.

When she returned home she expected to see Carp working on the campground, but his truck wasn't there. He was having problems with his truck, but Carp had told her he'd call if he couldn't get it started.

She went to the campground. Maybe someone had given him a ride. She went to the dorm where he was to work that day, but he wasn't there. From there she drove to his house. His truck was parked in the driveway. Getting out of her car, she walked to the door. A bite was definitely in the air and the weatherman predicted snow that evening. She hoped it was more than the scattering they'd received the last time. She was going to bring wood in for her fireplace, because there was nothing like a fire on a snowy day.

She knocked on Carp's door. It took five minutes of knocking before he responded. His eyes were bloodshot, he needed a shave and he'd slept in his clothes. Worse, he reeked of stale alcohol.

He was drunk.

"Carp, you promised." Noelle was really disappointed. He'd seemed to need the job as much as she needed a reliable carpenter.

He ran a hand across his face. "Sorry. Ran into a little trouble last night."

"I'll say you did."

He squinted against the bright light. "Got a headache."

"Well, you're looking in the wrong place if you expect me to know what to do." Noelle pushed open the door and went inside, heading straight to the kitchen. "Where's your coffee?" she asked.

He was sitting at the table holding his head in his hands. Carp was going to be no help—with either finding the coffee or getting any work done today.

"Why don't you take a shower while I fix coffee and breakfast?"

"Head hurts."

"It'll feel better after a shower. I'll look for some aspirin."

"You've never had a hangover."

"No, I've got more sense. Now go."

He lumbered off. A minute later she heard water running from a distance. Assured he was indeed taking his shower, she turned to prepare breakfast.

Noelle looked around his galley kitchen. It was large and he had little food in the fridge. At least there were a dozen eggs. She quickly checked the carton for an expiration date. Taking the eggs out, she started to search for a pan, but the kitchen was too messy to cook in.

She rolled up her sleeves. First she washed out the coffeepot, then she got the coffee going. She washed the dishes, wiped down the counter space and the small table tucked in the corner before she swept the floor. At least the floor had been mopped recently.

She found a can of corned beef hash in the

cabinet. By the time she fried it and the eggs, Carp came in the kitchen looking a thousand times better.

"Need aspirin," he said, sinking into a chair.

"Let's get some food in you first. I have eggs, corn beef hash and toast."

He groaned. "I don't think I can hold it down."

"Let's give it a try."

After she coaxed food and coffee into him, she said, "Feeling any better?"

"A little."

"I'm depending on you to get my camp ready for summer."

He sighed heavily. "I'm always letting people down. You can get just about anybody to do your work. Some people work pretty cheap. Why are you fooling around with me?"

She sensed there was story behind his alcoholism. She patted his hand. "I think you're being hard on yourself."

He shook his head.

"What happened?" she asked.

"My ex called last night. I spoke to the kids. I miss them so much. And then I got to feeling lonely. I took one sip." He shrugged as if to say the rest was history.

"I'm sorry, Carp. You ever thought about getting some help?"

"Thought about it. That's as far as it goes. I can stop if I want to."

"How often do you see your children?"

"Some holidays and a couple of weeks during the summer. It's not enough," he said.

"Where do they live?"

"In Baltimore."

"That's close enough for you to get them on some weekends."

"But they're involved in things. Sports and school activities."

"Tell you what. Call your ex. Tell her you want to see them at least once a month. It's not going to hurt them to miss one game. Or you can spend a weekend in Baltimore and have them stay with you there."

He seemed to perk up at the thought of seeing his children. "I'll try it."

Noelle could relate. She felt the same about seeing Colin tonight. Especially since she'd got a good glimpse of his body in swim trunks yesterday. Her heart still tripped when she thought of his hard, lean and gorgeous form.

Chapter 7

Colin found himself reaching for his phone. It seemed only a few hours had gone by without him thinking of calling Noelle, hearing her sweet voice. She got under his skin in the worst possible way. He should hang up the phone and tend to his work.

He failed to listen to his own lecture because he pressed the button to dial her number ten minutes later. *You are so whipped,* he berated himself. From the moment he'd met Noelle he'd stopped acting like the old Colin who had a string of women, but none who'd captured his attention enough for him to focus on her exclusively.

"Your brother get off okay?" he asked when she answered the phone.

"Yes," Noelle replied. "He should be home soon. He has to pack so Dad can take him back to school tomorrow." She gripped the phone tighter. "Is everything okay?"

"Yeah, yeah." He tried to lighten his voice.

"You sound angry. Are the horses okay? Maggie Girl?"

Colin took a deep breath. It wasn't her fault he'd lost his mind. On second thought, it was exactly her fault.

"So what are you doing today?" she asked in that soothing, sweet voice.

"Got a couple of horses coming. A boatload of paperwork is waiting for me. How's Carp working out?"

She sighed. "He had a little setback this morning, but he's working now."

"He's been drinking?"

"He's worried about his children, poor man. I fixed him breakfast and we talked. I think he's going to try to resolve visitation rights with his wife. That should help."

"You have a soft heart." His anger quickly dissipated in the face of her concern. "No wonder I knew working for you would be good for him. But you're going to have to keep an eye on him. Maybe it would have been a good idea to get a more reliable carpenter."

"I'm glad you recommended him. He'll work out okay. So, how is Mr. Avery?"

"I don't know." Other women he'd dated asked about George, but only because they thought it was the thing to do. He knew Noelle was genuinely concerned. She had heart. It was one of the things that appealed to him. "He doesn't take much interest in work anymore. He used to do a lot of the paperwork. Now it's kind of backing up. I'm playing catch-up."

"How sad. If there's anything I can do, let me know. If you want me to attend grief sessions with him, I'll go."

"I'll talk to him. Thanks for the offer. So what are you doing?"

"I'm writing a thank-you note to Leila. It was so nice of her to send the soup, and the tea yesterday was wonderful."

"Next time I hope she makes some man-size sandwiches. It took a thousand of those little things to fill me up." Leila had packed some for Noelle to take home and enough for Greg's trip home on the plane.

"They were perfect. I'm going to eat some of them for lunch."

"Well, she wants you to stop by if you're out. I think she's trying to fatten you up, or she wants to make sure I settle on you."

Noelle chuckled.

"I've already told her you're my one and only. So watch out. She's never liked any of my other girlfriends. She was always criticizing them, but she never criticizes you."

"Umm."

"I've got to go. Can't wait for tonight, baby."

Colin headed for the barn, but stopped in his tracks when he noticed his father's car approaching. Colin blew out a long breath. He'd been feeling pretty good till now. He waited outside for Leander to approach him.

"Surprised to see you here in the middle of the day," Colin said as his father exited the car.

Leander frowned. "We need to talk."

"Okay," Colin said slowly, frowning himself. "Why don't we go to the office?"

As they trooped to the office Colin wondered what brought his father out here this time.

He opened the office door and let Leander enter before him. They passed George's closed door on the way to Colin's office.

"Have a seat," he said, but his father took long

strides to the window and watched the activity outside the barn.

Colin liked his office. It was a huge space, big enough for a sitting area with a couch and a couple of chairs. From behind his expansive desk he had a view of the stables and the mountains behind. When he had to work indoors it gave him pleasure to be able to watch what was going on. The space had belonged to his grandfather, but the older man had turned it over to Colin a year before he'd died.

Leila had chosen the Persian rug. She'd also chosen some of the paintings on the wall and put a few plants in there that Colin often forgot to water. He didn't worry about it because Leila used the excuse of the plants to come to the office once a week. Usually she brought lunch with her.

His father still gazed out of the window and Colin wondered if he was thinking of his own father.

Leander was never still. Often Colin thought he got his energy from him, because he often caught himself pacing. But their tastes were 180 degrees apart. Everything Colin liked, his father disliked.

"What's going on?" Colin asked.

"I got a call from one of your creditors this morning. This is the loan Dad talked me into securing for the farm. You have a huge outstanding debt that should have been paid a month ago. They waited as long as they could, but finally called me."

Damn. Colin ran a hand over his head. "It must have been misplaced. I'll check on it and take care of it right away." George had told him he'd handled the bills, but George's mind wasn't really on his work. Colin tried to give him something to do so he wouldn't dwell on his son's death. He should have kept closer tabs on him, but his hands had been full with the farm.

His father frowned. "Are you sure the problem doesn't have more to do with the lack of funds?"

"We have enough money to take care of the bills."

"I should have sold my half of the farm right after Dad died."

"You know he didn't want that," Colin protested. "His dream was to make this a successful thoroughbred farm, the way it was years ago."

"And he spent the better part of his life throwing good money after bad to make that happen."

"That's not true. It's finally paying off. Yes, it took time. And it's part of a decision Grandpa made before he died. He wanted to build this farm up so it could sustain the lean years, and with Diamond Spirit we finally have a chance. Grandpa would want us to give him a chance to pull us into the black. I know he can do it."

"This entire farm is contingent on one horse. If something happens to Diamond Spirit tomorrow, you'll be up a creek."

"That's not true. We have horses that are racing in the money. We're getting good stud fees from several of our stallions, just not the draw of Diamond Spirit. You just have to give Maggie Girl a chance."

"By getting calls that the bills aren't being paid on time?"

"This is one that slipped though the cracks. I'll find it and pay it. I'll personally deliver the check to D.C. today."

"It's embarrassing. I have always paid my bills on time, and although this business has just about run itself into the ground, Dad always paid his, too."

"Don't worry, Dad. I'm not about to let that tradition go down the drain on my watch."

"See to it that you don't. I've told them to inform me if there are any more late payments."

Colin gritted his teeth. He was already putting in fourteen- to sixteen-hour days, barely giving him any time to stoke his relationship with Noelle. With his reputation, if he showed up any less, she'd think he was seeing other women. What she didn't know was that because of the grief his father was giving him about settling down, he'd cut back on women the last few months. Colin stifled a sigh. He'd either have to hire another employee or increase his hours.

"I can take care of my business, Dad."

"Then do it."

After his father left, Colin went to George's office. The older man had finally put in an appearance. He was sitting behind his desk staring into space. If his father sold his share of the farm, what would become of George? How would the new owner treat him? He wouldn't necessarily look out for George's welfare. George needed this place. This was the only home he'd known. His son had been born here, spent most of his life here. His wife had lived here.

Colin conjured up a smile he didn't feel. "How's it going?"

The older man jumped. "Fine, just fine. Was that Leander's car I saw outside?"

"Yes."

"Is he going to spend the night? Maybe I need to let Leila know to expect company."

"No, he has to get back to work."

George nodded.

"I'm looking for a bill." Colin named the company. "Have you seen it?"

A stack of papers was piled high on George's desk. He patted the stack. "I think it's in here somewhere. I haven't gotten to them yet."

"I think Leila mentioned lunch was ready. Why don't you go ahead? I'll be there as soon as I find this bill."

George motioned to the stack. "I need to take care of this before I leave town." He was heading to Florida for an important race.

"Don't worry about it. I'll take care of the stash," Colin said. "Go on and have your lunch. I'll try to join you in a few minutes."

"You sure?"

Colin nodded and got the man moving. George put his coat and hat on, wrapping his scarf around his neck. Leila had scolded him so much about that scarf, he now performed the duty by rote.

Colin sat in George's vacated chair and searched for the bill. It took him about five minutes to find it. He put it to the side and fingered through the rest of the papers. There were a lot of things that weren't being done. He'd have to go through them tomorrow.

He found the checkbook and wrote out a check. Then he slipped it with the bill into an envelope. He hated that hour-long drive to D.C., but there was no other option. He headed to his secretary's desk.

"I need you to go through the stack of bills on George's desk and get them ready for payment. Check on the ones that have and haven't been paid and leave the ones that haven't on my desk. I'll make out checks later on tonight."

"All right," the secretary said.

He dialed Noelle's number. "Hey, I have to run into D.C. Care to go with me? We could play tourists this afternoon, have dinner there tonight. How does a Moroccan restaurant sound?"

"Sounds great."

"Can you get away?"

"Sure."

"Pick you up in an hour. I'm going to have lunch with George first." Colin glanced at his watch. Just enough time for a quick shower, too. He needed it.

Noelle changed clothes and dabbed on a light-scented perfume before she drove to the camp.

She found Carp in one of the rooms. A kerosene lantern warmed the space as he worked. She leaned against the doorjamb, watching him for several minutes before he noticed her.

"Don't worry," he said, turning off his power saw. "I'm not drinking."

"I'm not checking up on you," she said. He

seemed to have recovered form his hangover. "I'm going into D.C. Will you be okay by yourself?"

"Sure. Listen, I'm really sorry about this morning. Won't happen again."

Noelle nodded. "Do you want me to take you home now? It'll be late before I return."

"No, I can get a ride. Don't worry about that. Have fun. Don't stay out too late, though. It's supposed to snow tonight."

"They've been talking about that for a while. I'm ready for it. Looking forward to it, actually. My first snow in a long time." She'd grown up in L.A., where it didn't snow, and had lived in Memphis, where it rarely snowed.

Carp chuckled. "Before winter's over you'll be tired of the slipping and sliding."

"It's half over already."

"Got to get through February. Don't eat that snow, now. Not like it was when I was a boy. There's all kinds of junk in the atmosphere. My mama used to make snow cream. It was delicious. Can't do that anymore."

"My mom used to tell me about that. She said her mother mixed vanilla and sugar in it."

"I don't know how Mama made it, but we always looked forward to the second snow. Couldn't eat the first snow. Mama said it cleaned the atmosphere." With a smile on his face, Carp picked up the power saw. "Gotta get back to work. You have fun now."

"I will."

As Noelle drove back home, she hoped she and Colin could watch the snow together. Maybe they could roast marshmallows and cuddle before a fire.

That sounded like a perfect way to spend an evening.

Traffic flowed steadily toward D.C. Colin turned the radio to an R&B station.

"I didn't see George," Noelle said.

"He's going to Florida to a race. I thought it'd do him good to get out of town for a few days. Brent's going, too. He'll pick him up from the airport and keep an eye on him."

It was interesting watching the change of terrain as they drew closer to D.C. There were more shopping areas and fewer trees.

In D.C. it only took Colin a few moments to deliver the check, and then he drove to the Mall and circled the block a few times before he found a parking space.

"I've made reservations for eight at Marrakesh," he said.

"I've heard of it."

"I'm sure you'll enjoy the belly dancer. Do you know how to belly dance?" he teased.

"No. Where are we going now?"

"Trying to change the subject?" he asked with a mischievous grin.

"Is it working?"

His mouth curved with tenderness. "They have a new exhibit on display at the Smithsonian I thought you'd like to see."

"Oh, yes."

They walked the Mall. Busloads of children were inside the museums. The wind had increased and Noelle pulled her coat tighter around her. Colin looped his arm around her drawing her close to his body heat.

Although Colin's mother had dragged him and his siblings to museums each year, he'd taken the experiences for granted as another thing they had to do for educational purposes. How many times had he heard her say how blessed they were to be so close to so much culture? It would be criminal not to take advantage of it, she'd remind them when they balked. But now he derived joy from Noelle's enthusiasm with the museums, and they didn't seem such a drag.

He took note of her as she talked to scientists in

the Natural History Museum—even learned a thing or two. He and Noelle were able to tour two museums before closing time.

An attendant parked the car as they entered the Marrakesh restaurant. They were seated on comfortable cushions.

"This is like sitting around a cocktail table in the dining room," Noelle said.

Colin nodded as they brought out the first serving. The traditional manner of eating was with one's fingers.

"Are you going to feed me?" Colin asked.

"You trust my fingers?" she asked as she tore off a bit of the egg-filled pastry dusted with powdered sugar and gently pressed it into his mouth. He caressed her fingers lightly with his teeth. Then he tore off a portion and fed it to her.

He rubbed the powered sugar off her lips with his thumb and kissed her gently. Her tongue ran lightly over her lips and his stomach clenched. He forcibly contained a moan. Powerful sexual need was roaring through him.

Making it through dinner was going to be tough, especially given the fact that he'd wanted her for what seemed like forever.

Alternately, throughout the meal, seated side by side, they fed themselves and each other.

"Did your brother get home okay?" He had to do something, say something to break the sexual stronghold strangling him.

"Yes, he called me after he arrived home. He was packing and my mom was in the background grilling him about me—especially about you." She laughed. Her whole face seemed to light up. "I can expect a visit from my father again soon." She sighed. "He's heard about your slam, bam, thank you ma'am reputation, by the way."

"You know me better, don't you?"

"I've known you two weeks. That doesn't cover a lifetime by any stretch of imagination."

"So does that mean you're still having second thoughts?"

"It means I'm going to go with the flow for a change. I don't expect you to give me more than you're capable of."

Her statement twisted a knife in Colin's gut. Yes, in the past it was true he hadn't taken women seriously. But he thought Noelle believed that he'd changed. He needed her to believe him.

Colin pulled back and leaned against the cushion. "Look, the fact that I haven't found a woman I could be serious with in the past has no reflection on you."

"Colin, you don't have to explain yourself. You don't have to make promises. I'm willing to accept what you're willing to give. You don't have to commit yourself to me for life. The only promise I want is that you don't see other women when you're dating me. When you've had enough, you can leave with no tears, no recriminations. My eyes are wide open."

As if he couldn't be trusted to be responsible. As if he was still operating like a kid and not as an adult. Her lack of trust hurt. But he wouldn't reveal his feelings.

She was saying her eyes were wide open, but not her heart. You didn't fall in love with a man you couldn't trust. He tried to control his consternation as he thought it through. He was laying himself wide open for a woman who wasn't completely open herself. And maybe he deserved that. Maybe this was penance for the way he'd treated women in the past.

Just then the waiter brought the next course.

"Eat before your food gets cold," Colin told her. But he'd completely lost his appetite.

It wasn't the belly dancing that stirred Colin as much as the thought of Noelle gyrating her hips beneath him. He should still be angry with her. She'd insulted him, but he could barely catch his breath on their drive back to Middleburg. Even with the absence of traffic, that drive seemed too long.

Colin took Noelle's hand in his. He stopped at a red light on Route 50 in Middleburg, leaned over the console and kissed her with hunger and frustration. It would take time for her to trust him and he'd give her the time. His problem was that he'd never cared before, it had always been take it or leave it.

He couldn't leave Noelle. And that scared the pants off him.

A horn beeped behind them. Colin righted himself and drove on.

"It's snowing," Noelle said with the delight of a kid.

"You're going to see plenty before spring," Colin warned.

"We have to make a fire. I carried wood in earlier. I even have marshmallows to roast."

"It's just snow," Colin said, chuckling, but it was a joy to watch her delight with a simple act of nature.

"We're supposed to get five inches. We can have a snowball fight and make snow angels."

"Yeah. Ever been in a snowball fight?"

Candice Poarch

"A long time ago when we visited my grandparents at Christmas."

Colin pulled into the grocery-store parking lot. "We're going to have to do this up right for you."

Inside he selected some items, including chocolate and graham crackers. With her marshmallows, he had the ingredients for making s'mores.

The line was long and it took them awhile to get through, but Noelle didn't seem to mind. She kept looking out the window hoping the snow would gather faster.

Colin called his trainer and told him to call him on his cell if needed.

By the time they made it outside, there was a white coating on the ground.

"It takes forever for it to accumulate," Noelle moaned.

Colin couldn't help laughing. "When you have to drive home in it, you'll appreciate that. You're as happy as the kids. No school for them tomorrow."

They were in the close confines of the car again. Big, soft flakes fell silently to the ground. Noelle wondered why he didn't start the engine.

"I want you, Noelle. Tonight." He brushed her hair from her face.

She could only nod silently. His words had stolen her breath.

He leaned over and brushed her lips with his, then eased his tongue into her mouth. His taste was arousing.

Car lights flickered across them, and slowly they separated. Colin started the motor and with anticipation, they rode to her house. Silently they left his car, and Noelle noticed the snow had finally begun to accumulate. She opened the house door and suddenly she was nervous. She'd wanted Colin for so long.

"I'm going to keep you in bed so long that two feet of snow will be on the ground before I let you up."

"Promise?" Noelle asked, hurrying up the stairs in front of him. From the top of the stairs to her room seemed endless. All Colin could think about was getting those clothes off her and getting a glimpse of her naked skin.

Colin was overcome with conflicting emotions. He wanted to wait until she believed in him more, but he wanted her so badly he couldn't wait. He put his reservations on the back burner. She'd come around, he assured himself. He'd prove that he was here to stay.

She backed into the room, pulling him after her.

She flipped a switch that flooded the room with bright light.

Her V-neck sweater had driven him crazy all evening. He brushed his fingers across her cheek before his mouth descended on hers. He pulled her close to his body, wrapped his arms around her and held her close. Her warm breasts pressed against his chest, causing him to groan deep in his throat.

She tasted as sweet as a dream. What he was sharing with her was new and special. More than anything, he wanted to make this memorable for her. He wanted to please her as she'd never been pleasured before.

He pulled away from her, gathered the hem of her sweater and tugged it over her head to reveal the sweetest red camisole and matching bra.

"Red compliments your skin to perfection," he said in an unrecognizably husky voice.

She only smiled, but he glimpsed it momentarily before he tugged her back into his arms. His patience wore thin and he found himself kissing her from her lips to her breasts. He tugged the camisole over her head and then got rid of the bra. He sucked a deep breath when he got his first glimpse of her naked breasts.

He swirled his tongue slowly around her nipple

before he drew it into his mouth. Her moan was like music to his ears.

"You're gorgeous," he said. "Everywhere."

She grasped his sweater and tugged it over his head. Then she unbuttoned his shirt and he shrugged out of it.

He lifted her and carried her to the bed, pulled the covers back and placed her in the center. He peeled her jeans off her hips and her scrap of panties with it.

"Thought you'd be a thong girl," he teased.

"They're uncomfortable."

"I don't need them when I have a feast before my eyes." He kissed the length of her, taking his time. From her tiny gasps, he knew she was enjoying his touch as much as he enjoyed pleasuring her. He caressed her long legs, drew his tongue up the inside of her trembling thighs. Her hands tangled in his hair, stroked his shoulder, wherever she could reach.

"Are you ready for me, baby?" he asked, at the end of his endurance.

"Yes!"

And then he shucked his jeans and briefs and pulled on a condom.

Noelle felt the breath catch in her throat. Colin

was driving her to the edge of madness. She'd never, ever in her entire life felt this intense need before. Her body felt so hot, she was like a firecracker ready to explode.

His body was perfect, sculpted and strong, from his broad shoulders to his lean waist, then lower still... Her breath caught at the size of him. He hovered over her a moment, drawing her gaze. She was afraid of what he was seeing in her eyes. Then she felt his weight pressing her into the mattress, and his erection stretching her open. She felt like a flower blossoming for him.

And then he was sinking into her, filling her completely. Her body convulsed around him and they were moving together, her hands clutching his back, smoothing down to his backside and pressing him tighter to her.

He kissed her deeply, his tongue thrusting into her mouth. She savored each second of this experience. Even though she wasn't a virgin, she'd never been given this care before. She'd never felt so vulnerable, so fulfilled. He grasped her hips in his hands, plunging more deeply into her, increasing the pleasurable sensations.

He increased the pace, set their rhythm like practiced dancers as they moved together in harmony.

Their lips parted and he gazed directly in her eyes. She felt vulnerable as if he was seeing right into her deepest core.

Her body moved in rhythm with his as if they were one.

The whimperings coming from Noelle's lips let him know she was enjoying this as much as he was. He was caught off guard at the depth of his feelings for her.

And then her legs tightened around him, the tempo of her movements increased and she called out his name and clenched him tightly.

Only seconds later, he sank deeper into her on his own climax.

Chapter 8

The last thing Colin wanted to do was leave the warmth and softness of Noelle's body. What he *really* wanted to do was make love with her again and sleep with her tucked snugly in his arms, only to awaken in the morning to make love again.

Now he had more reason than ever to succeed on the farm. That reason was sleeping soundly in his arms. He tightened his arms around her and kissed her beneath her ear, then on her soft cheek before he eased himself from her bed and dressed quietly. He gazed at her snuggled comfortably under the covers before he left the room and let himself outside.

It had snowed two inches already. The cold air slapped him as snowflakes swirled around. He started the truck and let the engine warm while he used the scraper to clean the snow from the windows.

It was almost one in the morning when Colin drove away and made his way to the office to start leafing through unpaid bills. Casey had done a good job of setting things up for him.

Usually George was on top of the bills, got their proper documentation to the accountant and paid everything on time. He wanted to know where every cent was going or coming in. Now he no longer cared.

It was almost three-thirty by the time Colin made it to bed.

Morning came all too quickly. He hit his alarm and slept till six, when the scent of Leila's coffee wafted in the air.

He was feeling on top of the world, as if he had energy to spare. He sang in the shower and as he dressed. Leila was humming as he bounded down the stairs. She had fixed a nice spread.

"How was your date yesterday?" she asked with a sly smile as she rolled dough. "Must have tired you out. You don't usually sleep in."

"It was very good."

"You got in late."

Colin threw her a lazy glance. "Leila, are you keeping tabs on me?"

"Don't I always?"

Colin chuckled.

"I'm making my special chicken salad for lunch, the recipe you like."

"I'll be here at twelve sharp, not a second later," he said.

"The salad is for Noelle. You can eat some leftovers from the fridge," she teased. She set the dough aside to rise and placed a towel over the pan. "I'll slice some bread for you to take to Noelle, too," she continued.

Colin grabbed Leila around the waist and kissed her soundly on the cheek. "While your leftovers are always delicious, your chicken salad is my favorite."

"Oh, you go on with your foolishness, boy. You're going to make my dough fall."

"It wouldn't dare," Colin said.

"Always knew how to wrap me around your finger."

Chuckling, she started walking from the room. "Eat before your food gets cold."

Colin filled his plate and sat at the table, still basking in his night of lovemaking.

* * *

Noelle slept through the night and woke slowly the next morning—completely naked and alone. Heat and desire stole over her when she thought of the previous night's lovemaking.

She wondered when Colin had left during the night. Perhaps he'd waited until early morning.

Snow. It had snowed the night before, she remembered. Smiling, she hopped out of bed and ran to the window. It was a picture-perfect winter wonderland just like the scene on a Christmas card.

Tearing herself from the view, she searched through the drawer for a camera. She'd have to send pictures to Greg and her parents. She couldn't wait to be out in it.

Quickly she showered and dressed, tugging on her new lined boots and donning her gloves.

It was cold. Her feet crunched in the snow as she walked down the steps. Her car was covered with it, so she gathered some in her hand and patted it into a ball. She was disappointed she had no one to toss it at.

The wind was blowing and she felt the chill against her face. In minutes she saw a truck coming up her lane. It was Carp. Coming to a stop, he hopped out.

"What're you doing out here in the cold when you don't have to be?" he asked, rubbing his hands together.

"I love the snow."

"You'll get tired of it before March. Thought I'd stop by and make sure you were all right before I went to the camp."

"You're going to work in the snow?"

"Snow doesn't bother me. I'm working inside. Gonna fire up that lantern and I'll be toasty."

"Would you like some hot chocolate before you go?"

"No. Got a big thermos of hot coffee to keep my insides warm. You take care. If you need anything just holler." Carp got into his truck and started off. Tires crunched on the snow as he drove toward the campsite, his tire tracks the only thing marring the smooth surface.

Noelle went back inside. First she started a fire in the fireplace, then she made hot chocolate to warm herself before she prepared eggs and sausage for breakfast.

She looked at the time. It was eight and Colin hadn't called. He must be very busy.

With so much to do, Noelle didn't need to while away the hours thinking of Colin. After breakfast she unpacked the boxes with materials related to the campground. Next week she was going to begin work on the camp full-time. She was deep into filing papers in the file cabinet by the time her doorbell rang. She was surprised and very pleased to see Colin at the door. What on earth had brought him here in the middle of the day?

Smoothing her hair back with her hand, she opened the door.

"Hi," Colin said in a low, intimate voice just before he kissed her. His lips were cool in contrast to the warmth of his mouth. His heat radiated through her body.

"Missed you," he said.

"It's only been a few hours."

"Still missed you. Leila sent lunch," he said with a devilish grin. "I want some, too."

"How kind of her. I'm sure she sent enough for two."

"I want something else for lunch."

Noelle's face heated.

"Go put on your coat, boots, gloves and scarf. We're going to play in your winter wonderland."

Noelle didn't question what had brought Colin here. She was glad he was with her.

In minutes she'd donned the clothes and was

outside. Colin had cleaned most of the snow off her car windows. She went around the other side to help him. She barely had time to lift her arms before he called her name.

The first snowball that hit her square in the face was a shock. She shrieked.

Colin pelted her a couple of more times with snowballs before she gathered up a handful of snow to form her own and toss it at him. This was war. Although she volleyed back and forth she soon discovered she was no match for his strength.

"Truce! Truce!" she finally called out, laughing.

He approached her, kissed her on the lips. She took the snow in her hands and smashed it into his cheeks.

"No fair." And then they were on the ground rolling in the snow like a couple of kids.

As Colin lay on top of Noelle, her laughing face smiling up at him, he felt as if angels had smiled down on him. He rolled so that she was now on top of him, and the cold was against his back. He lost his smile and saw the smile slowly fade from her face to leave a warm glow. He pressed her face close to his and placed a soft kiss on her lips. He'd meant only a light kiss, but once he tasted her, he couldn't let go. Their tongues teased and mated. He ran his hands down her back, feeling the impression of her through her coat. His hand roamed back to her head, pressing her closer. Time and temperature had no meaning.

It seemed ages had passed before they parted at last and the cold began to seep in. "Ice is dripping down my neck," Noelle said.

"So much for the pleasure of snow," Colin muttered.

"I will always remember this—" she peppered his face with kisses "—and you—" she kissed his lips this time "—when I think of snow."

Colin had never, ever been this content, this happy, this pleased. "Let's go inside."

She stood and they ran inside and peeled off their cold, damp clothes.

"I'll put yours in the dryer so you can leave soon."

"I'm not leaving anytime soon."

"But George—"

"They can reach me if they need me."

After they stripped down to their undies, Noelle put the wet clothes in the dryer.

Colin put more wood on the fire and urged it to a full blaze while Noelle made more hot chocolate. He put the ingredients for s'mores together.

"I'll put them in the oven when we're ready to eat them. They're better hot."

Noelle had donned a housecoat.

"I don't have anything big enough for you. So will this blanket do?" She held up a pink blanket.

"Pink?" He laughed. "I'll cover myself with anything if you snuggle up in it with me."

So they ate their lunch in the living room in front of the fire. Colin melted the s'mores in the oven. When he took the pan out, they fed the treats to each other. When some got on Noelle's lip, he licked it off.

"This is decadent," Colin said. "And you're naughty. I'm usually working."

"Umm, this is better."

She put thick blankets and pillows on the rug and they stretched out on them. Colin gritted his teeth. If he didn't make love to her soon, he was going to go out of his mind.

He watched the light from the fire play across her face.

He had to take it slower this time. He was so eager to be inside her, the last time had been hurried. But not this time. He inhaled a sharp breath and blew it out slowly.

Leisurely, he caressed her body from head to foot. He kissed her, ran his lips and tongue over her curves until she was straining for release—and he gave it to her. He caressed her intimately until she sang out in complete fulfillment.

He stroked her gently and built her desire to a pressure point again.

She slowly stroked him as she slid the condom on. He gritted his teeth to keep from exploding. Then he slid into her. She was moist and ready. Sensations rushed through him. They moved in sync as if a choreographer had arranged their steps, and when they climaxed, it was as explosive as the first time.

For minutes, Colin couldn't move. She'd wrenched every ounce of strength out of him. Then he moved to her side and placed his arms around her.

This was something new and exciting for Colin, even a little scary, given the extent he was allowing himself to be vulnerable. He trusted Noelle. For the first time, he trusted a woman enough to change.

Colin pulled the covers up around them. He kissed her, then settled back on the pillow. She snuggled up under him and he liked that. He could get used to this really fast.

Contented, they slept with the fire crackling in front of them.

For the first time in his life, Colin was in love.

***

Colin woke up when the cell phone rang. Thinking it was his, he picked it up absentmindedly and pressed the talk button.

"Noelle. It's about time you answered your phone. I've been calling and calling you. Why haven't you returned my calls?" It was Cindy Jamison, and she was talking so rapid-fire he couldn't identify himself. And Noelle, he noticed now, wasn't beside him. "I hear it's snowing there. You must love that. But I need to talk to you, girl. Mr. Avery was talking to Dad and he seems to think you and Colin are a couple. Didn't I tell you to stop? Why aren't you listening? Mr. Avery likes you. Now that you're on the farm, you need to break off that relationship with Colin. It wasn't supposed to go this far. What's wrong with you? I worry about you, girl. You don't need him anymore. He's bad news and you know he's a player. But as usual I suspect you're being hardheaded."

She paused then, but Colin couldn't speak. "Noelle…Noelle? Are you listening to me?"

Colin hung up.

His heart fell into his stomach. He sat frozen in place. He'd been the worst kind of fool. And like a fool, he'd fallen in love with Noelle—and she was playing him. Why? To get on the farm? And what was her connection to George?

Leaving the blanket on the floor he went searching for her. Looking graceful and beautiful in lounging pajamas, she came down the stairs like some fifties movie star. He waited for her at the foot. Her smile set his teeth on edge.

"You're finally up. You must have really been tired," she said. She smelled sweet, as if she'd used scented soap.

"Who are you and why are you here?" he asked bluntly.

Clearly puzzled, she tilted her head slightly to the side. "What?"

"Why are you here?" he repeated. "Why did you use me to get on the farm?"

"What are you talking about?" she asked. "Why are you asking me this?"

"Stop the innocent act. There have been enough lies between us. If you wanted something, why didn't you come right out and ask? Are you here to destroy one of the animals, or to destroy the farm?"

"Of course not," Noelle said. "Why would you even think such a thing?"

"Because people are paid to do those things. So if you're not here to destroy us, why *are* you here?

Because it certainly isn't because you love me," he sneered.

"Just tell me why you are asking me this," she repeated.

"Your friend Cindy wants you to leave me the heck alone because you got what you were after."

"Cindy?" She closed her eyes briefly. "Oh my gosh."

"I answered your cell phone thinking it was mine."

She sighed. Silence followed, before she said, "It's not like that, Colin. I wasn't playing games with you. I never expected to feel this way about you. I would have gotten on the farm without your assistance. My grandparents were friends with the Averys."

"Stop beating around the bush."

"There's nothing to tell."

"And that's your answer? After all we've been through? After all we've shared, that's all you have to say?"

"It has nothing to do with you."

He shook his head to clear it. Didn't last night mean anything to her? How could she tell him it had nothing to do with him? Time seemed to stand still as he stared at her before he told her, "You're not welcome on the farm any longer. Don't come back, because you won't be admitted." He moved down the hall to the dryer and quickly dragged on his clothes. Then he slammed out the door without saying another word to her.

Damn it. He couldn't believe this. The one time he'd let his guard down, it was with someone who was only using him. The vibes were all one-sided.

Stomach roiling, Colin slammed into his truck and drove the couple of miles to his house. He hit the wheel. Damn it. He'd known it had to be too good to be true. Anger hurt less than pain. He wouldn't let himself go there yet.

She was only pretending to like him. How could she make love to him like that and pretend? What kind of woman was she? And why had she been hanging out at Brent's place? Why hadn't Brent warned him? Obviously he hadn't known what kind of woman his daughter was bringing home. After all, Colin had known Brent for a long time. The man didn't suffer fools.

The last thing Colin wanted to do was sit at his desk and do paperwork, but it had to be done. Sensing his bad mood, his secretary had taken one look at him and closed his office door. But his curtains were open and he saw William's SUV pull into the drive.

Voices mingled outside his office. Colin could only hope the secretary had William on his way, but then he heard a knock at his door before it opened. The woman peeked in.

"Mr. Bowden is here to see you." She left and William sauntered in. Colin leaned back in his chair.

"I hear Uncle George is in Florida," William said.

"He is."

"Came by to see if he'd come home with me for a couple of weeks. Spend some time with Mama."

"He doesn't like to leave the farm except for races," Colin said.

William looked around his office. "I also got a buyer who's interested in this place."

"Did he ask you to find him a buyer?"

"He's not doing much here," William said with a smug look.

"Why don't you just leave him alone? We both know you're only here for what you can get. You don't give a damn about George."

William quirked an eyebrow. "And you do?"

"Yeah, I care."

"You think you own this place with Uncle George out of commission? Things are set up just the way you want them, aren't they? But let me give you a warning. Uncle George isn't going to be handling this for long. And who do you think will eventually handle his affairs? Me, that's who. Uncle George owns fifty-one percent of this place. You won't be able to do squat without my permission."

Colin stood, shoving his chair back. "You don't own shit now, so get the hell off this property before I throw you off."

"I'm going. But you'll have to deal with me one day." He grinned his slick snake-oil-salesman grin. Colin wanted to pop it right off his face. "And I can't wait." Turning on his heels he left the office without a word to the secretary. Once outside, he gazed back through the window at Colin before he got in his truck and drove away, leaving behind the pall of his dire warnings.

If George didn't pull himself together, Colin wouldn't put it past William to have him declared unfit.

Night had fallen. For most of the day, Noelle had run on self-righteous anger. After all she and Colin had shared, didn't he know her at all? How could he believe she'd destroy his animals or do anything to harm the farm?

She ached with disappointment and regret. She couldn't tell him the reason she was here. This was one she couldn't win. If she told him George was her grandfather he'd accuse her of being another money grabber like William and the woman who'd pretended she was George's granddaughter.

It didn't take long for the anger to completely abate and for acute loss to stab her. She'd fallen for Colin in the worst possible way. Which was why she couldn't leave him the way Cindy kept encouraging her to do.

Her phone rang and she answered it immediately.

"What the heck is going on? Why didn't you respond when I called you?" Cindy asked. "I'm talking into thin air and the phone disconnects."

"Bad connection." Noelle didn't see any sense in explaining things to Cindy. Her and her big mouth. But it wasn't Cindy's fault.

"How is it going with lover boy?"

"It's not."

"I'm glad you finally ended that," Cindy said with apparent relief. "How's the snow?"

"Beautiful." Noelle wanted to cry after her beautiful morning of play and lovemaking. Colin had taken the day off to spend with her. A precious day when his work meant so much to him.

"I saw Mr. Avery at the track. He had dinner with us last night. I couldn't help noticing that you have his eyes," Cindy was saying. "He's a nice man, Noelle."

"Yes, he is. Uh, Cindy, I have to go. I'm sleepy. It's late."

"Oh, sorry. But you never went to bed early."

"I've been working hard. As soon as I get the time I'll call, okay?"

Sinking onto the couch and holding the blanket to her face to get a whiff of Colin, Noelle shut her phone. She didn't feel like talking to anyone right now. The bottom line was, she'd hurt Colin and she never meant to do that. He didn't deserve that.

All day she'd tried to come up with a solution to her dilemma. She owed Colin an explanation even if he thought she was after George's money. She dialed Colin's cell phone, but was immediately thrown into voice mail. She hung up. Ten minutes later she called again. This time she left a message apologizing and asked him to call her.

That night, when Noelle got into bed, she smelled Colin on the sheets. She should change them, but she missed him.

Hugging his pillow tight against her chest, she knew she'd never be able to sleep tonight. She got up and inserted an action movie in her DVD player. She couldn't stand to watch a romance.

With reception on only a couple of channels on TV she really did have to call the satellite people.

While waiting for Colin to return her call, Noelle fell asleep, her cell phone within reach on the bedside table.

After William left, Colin went to the stables and worked until he was too tired to do anything except shower and fall into bed. His workers had kept a weary distance. Even the horses had picked up on his sour disposition.

He'd felt his employees watching him as he mucked stalls—something he rarely did anymore—and worked beside them. The usual chatter had been missing. He'd heard only the nickers from the animals. He'd needed the physical labor. He thought he'd worked it out of his system until he'd exited the barn around one that morning and crunched through the snow.

He'd cursed under his breath, got in his truck and driven home. Why the hell hadn't anyone cleared the path yet? He'd been tempted to get somebody out of bed. Suddenly, reason set in. He couldn't take his temper out on the employees.

Yet now, unable to sleep, he lay in bed staring at the ceiling. Noelle had tried to reach him several times, but he didn't want to talk to her.

He started to drift off until he pictured her face smiling down at him in the snow. The image brought him wide awake again. And suddenly he was thinking of them making love for the first time, and of loving each other in front of the fireplace.

Damn. Would she ever stop plaguing his mind? He punched the pillow and lay back down.

Why the heck was he working himself half to death? William had been on the money. He'd get control of George's property eventually. And he'd sell it.

Noelle awakened around six the next morning. Glancing at her phone, she saw that Colin hadn't returned her call.

She got up, showered and dressed for the day. She wasn't really hungry, but she ate cereal anyway.

Carp came by at seven. He pulled his hat off. "Wanted to tell you, the electrician is coming by today. He's going to look over all the buildings."

"They have to be a mess after all these years."

"That about nails it."

"How are you doing, Carp?"

"Better than ever. I talked to my ex last night. To the kids, too. Told her I was coming to town on the weekend. She said the kids had games, but I asked if I could take them. And she agreed."

"I'm so happy for you."

"I haven't broached the possibility of them spending some weekends with me, but that's a start."

"A good start."

"Kind of looking forward to seeing my boy play basketball. My daughter's a cheerleader. Think I'm going to town to pick out some presents for them," he said, clearly looking forward to the event. "Been getting a lot of work done. I have to hire a couple of guys to help out for a few days, but I should be able to do most of it on my own."

Noelle nodded.

"Weatherman's talking about more snow next week. Hope it doesn't snow any more before the weekend."

Noelle didn't want to hear about snow. "Let me get you a cup of coffee to warm you up before you go back out there."

"I'd appreciate that. Colder today than usual."

"Come on in the kitchen and warm up. Why don't you have breakfast with me?"

"Coffee will do. I ate earlier."

She poured him a cup then got out a thermos and filled it.

"Thanks," he said and left. "I'll drop this by on my way home."

Noelle glanced outside. She hoped the roads were plowed well enough for her to drive her car. She bundled up in her coat and left for the farm. Obviously it was the only way she'd talk to Colin.

Unaccustomed to driving on snow, Noelle drove cautiously. A couple of times she was so slow her car eased backward down the hill. She realized she had to give it some gas to make it up. Puttering along, she was almost at the ranch when she slid into a ditch.

Just what she needed.

She tried to reach Colin again, but, of course, he wouldn't pick up. Leaving her hazard lights on, she got out of the car and walked the rest of the way to the ranch.

She waved to the guard and kept walking past, but he stopped her.

"Excuse me?"

She'd spoken to him every time she came through.

"Sorry, ma'am. Orders." He looked apologetically at her. "I can't let you in."

"Well, will you call Colin and tell him I need to

talk to him? And please let me know if he's coming. After I call AAA to get my car out the ditch, I'm walking back to it."

When he closed the door to radio up to the house, Noelle dialed Information for the number for AAA. She was dialing the number when the guard opened the window.

"We'll get you out of the ditch, ma'am. AAA will take hours getting here. When it snows, seems like a million cars need help," the man said.

Five minutes later a closed-cab tractor came lumbering down the lane followed by a pickup truck. The tractor stopped beside her.

"Where're you stuck?" the man asked.

"About a mile down the road," she said, tightening the coat around her. Her body clearly wasn't acclimated to this weather yet. She wondered if it would ever be. She felt half-frozen. The lining in her boots did little to warm her toes.

The tractor drove on, but the truck stopped beside her. A thin, wiry looking brown-skinned man with a roadmap of wrinkles on his face lowered the window. "Hop in," he called out.

Opening the door, Noelle eagerly got into the warm cab and rolled the window up. "Whoo. Really cold out there."

He grinned. "That it is, ma'am."

"It's much warmer in here. Thank you. Where's Colin?" Noelle asked. Why hadn't he come to pick her up? She needed to talk to him.

"He's occupied right now. Said he'll get back to you later." The man's face darkened in embarrassment. Colin had probably given him an earful of choice words about her in the meantime.

Well, if he wanted to act stupid and refuse to talk to her, there was nothing she could do but let him stew. She was angry herself by now.

"Give him a message for me, please?" she said as sweet as she could manage.

"Sure, ma'am. Be glad to. What is it?"

"Tell him to drop dead."

The man threw his head back and laughed. "I like you. I think he's met his match. Finally. You've got spunk." He extended a hand. "I'm Ron by the way."

His hand nearly swallowed hers.

"Been on the farm a long time," he said. "Knew Colin since he was a little one. And I've got to say I'm very pleased to meet you."

Noelle smiled.

When they approached her car, the man on the tractor was hooking a chain to it.

"Give me your keys," Ron said. "You stay in the truck where it's warm and toasty. We'll have you out of the ditch in no time. The road's a slippery devil right now."

Noelle handed over her keys and a blast of cold air rushed in when Ron exited the truck. He hunched his shoulders against the cold. But inside, he'd left the heater on and she was quickly warm again.

The men worked quickly and within minutes they had her car out of the ditch. Ron entered the cab rubbing his hands together. He slipped her a piece of paper with a telephone number. "Just in case you get stuck again. You drive home carefully, hear? And as soon as the weather breaks, get yourself some all-weather or snow tires." He nodded toward her car. "What you have now isn't worth crap in this weather."

"Thanks, Ron."

Once he drove away, Noelle realized there was no sense in going back to the farm. The guard would only tell her to move on.

She decided to head home. By now she was really ticked off with Colin. Maybe she hadn't been completely up front in the beginning, but her feelings for him were real. The least he could do was hear her explanation, not that that was going to ingratiate her with him.

Chapter 9

Drop dead. Ron had the nerve to laugh in Colin's face. "She's got spunk," he said.

"You got her out of the ditch okay?" Colin asked, ignoring his comment about spunk. He was tired and sleepy. He'd finally fallen asleep when it was almost time to get up.

"Took no time at all. She was nearly frozen by the time we got to the guard stand. Had her standing outside. Why would he do a thing like that? Not like she's a stranger."

Anybody else would have gotten fired for taking

such liberties, but the wiry old geezer figured he'd been there long enough to speak his mind.

"She looked okay, didn't she?" Colin was stupid enough to ask.

"Damn. If she'da looked any better I woulda had to turn the heater off."

Frustrated, Colin glared at the smart-mouthed old man. "George isn't here, but I can still fire you."

His only response was an outright laugh and shake of the head.

"Think you can contain yourself enough to pick up George from the airport?" Colin said.

Backing up, Ron held up his weathered arthritic fingers. "On my way," he said.

"Check and make sure she got home okay, will you?" He could have kicked himself, but the words materialized before he could check them. He shouldn't give a damn.

"Will do," Ron said. "Got to go that way anyway." Shaking his head, the older man shut the door behind him, but Colin heard him talking to the secretary on his way out. They both laughed before the outer door opened and closed.

Why the heck had Noelle been out driving in the snow on a day like today, anyway? Showing up on his turf only to get herself stuck in the ditch and then she'd told him to drop dead? She had some kind of nerve.

And after the pep talk he'd given himself to get her out of his system, she came right back like a stray cat that didn't know when to quit.

He donned his coat and gloves. "I'm leaving," he told his secretary. "You can reach me on my cell phone."

Noelle was sitting in front of the fireplace reading a book and sipping a cup of hot chocolate when her doorbell rang. She felt the cold all the way to her bones when she answered it.

She hadn't expected Colin to show up at all.

"Oh, so you finally decided to respond?" She went back to the sofa and sat, wrapping the blanket around herself.

Gritting his teeth, Colin entered the room slowly, shutting the door behind him.

"What did you want?" he asked.

"Excuse me?"

"You called a thousand times."

"Right now I want to hit you."

"I wouldn't advise it."

"I called to discuss Cindy's call. I'm not here to hurt the farm in any way. Yes, I had planned to meet you while you were in Memphis, but not to date you. Things got out of hand."

"You brought me over here to tell me that?"

Noelle reminded herself she was dealing with a man and his stupid pride.

"I wanted to meet George."

"Why?"

There was no option but to tell him the entire tale. "I'm the product of artificial insemination. Mackenzie was my donor father."

Colin laughed. Roared, actually. Noelle really wanted to sock him this time.

When the laughter subsided he wiped the moisture from his eyes. "I have to give it to you, lady. William needs to take lessons from you. You get on the inside, get the lay of the land, so to speak, before you broach George. You're a lot smarter than the other woman."

"I am not lying. Mackenzie Avery is my donor father. My mother conceived by artificial insemination when Mackenzie was in vet school in California. She asked him to be the donor and he complied. He gave me the right to contact him when I turned eighteen, but my mother didn't tell me that until years later. I put off contacting him for a while. You see, I had a dilemma. Franklin Greenwood is my father, a great father. I didn't want to make a move that would upset him."

Noelle took a swallow of chocolate for fortification. Then she warmed her hands around the cup. At least Colin was listening, had stopped that stupid grinning.

"Last May I called Mackenzie. I didn't know what to say. He made it easy, he kept the conversation going. Told me about his father and that he didn't have any other children. He told me about his veterinary practice. He said he wanted to meet me, and of course, I wanted to meet him." She took another swallow of chocolate.

"He was coming to see me the week he died." Tears ran down her face. Before she knew it, Colin was holding her in his arms. Mackenzie had died on his drive to the airport to catch a plane to Memphis.

"It was an accident. It wasn't your fault."

"But—"

"No buts. You don't have that power."

She took a tissue and blew her nose.

"Is he Gregory's father, too?"

"No. Dad's Greg's natural father."

Colin wouldn't get into that. "You have to tell George," he said.

"He'll hate me."

"He needs you. He needs a reason to go on." Colin didn't know why he believed her, but he did. He still hated the way she'd used him to meet George.

From the depth of her eyes he glimpsed wariness. "So you believe me."

"Of course I do. Why would you lie about a thing like that?"

"I wouldn't."

"If you had just told me, I would have helped you," he said. "But it's all water under the bridge."

"I wasn't going to say anything at all. I just wanted to meet him. That's all. Maybe get updated medical information." She sighed deeply. "Who am I fooling? I wanted to know if I took after him. If I looked like him or...I don't know. If there were pictures of his ancestors I favored. And then you told me about the vultures circling and I knew I could never tell him."

"George will answer all your questions."

As much as Colin wanted to hold on to his anger he couldn't. Their relationship was over, and God help him, he still had strong feelings for her, but this wasn't about him. Then he realized he hadn't completely purged his anger; it was still there, lingering beneath the surface. But George was suffering. He needed to know.

"We have to tell George," Colin repeated.

"I'm not ready."

"I never took you for a coward. George needs you."

Noelle inhaled deeply. "Okay."

"He should be home from the airport soon. I'll come back to get you."

"Thanks, Colin, for making this easier."

He smiled and let himself out.

Colin left because he couldn't stay in the same house, in the same room as Noelle, without wanting her. And he couldn't bring her with him and have her at the barn disturbing his peace. Or in the house with Leila clucking over her.

If he'd thought it was bad before, once George found out she was his granddaughter, he'd never see the last of her.

Colin drove back to the farm grateful there was always enough work to do on a thoroughbred farm to keep his mind occupied.

"Noelle," Leila said when she answered the door later that day. "I'm so pleased to see you again."

"Where's George, Leila?" Colin asked, coming in right behind Noelle.

"In the den. He's a bit tired from the trip."

Noelle was nervous as Colin led her into the den where a cozy fire burned in the fireplace.

"Hello, there," George said, standing. "Nice to see you again, Noelle."

Noelle gave him a nervous smile.

"How was your trip, George?" Colin asked.

"Florida is nice, but it's good to be back home. We placed well, though."

While they talked shop, Noelle perused the pictures around the room. There were many of Mackenzie at different ages, starting from the time he was a baby.

Mackenzie had his father's eyes, she realized. Her eyes. They must be a strong family trait. There were pictures of George's wife, too. Noelle remembered very little of the woman, though she'd been alive when Noelle visited her grandparents.

She placed the photo back on the table and stood by the window.

"Have a seat, George," Colin said, leading him to a wingback chair.

She joined Colin on the couch.

"What's going on?" George asked.

Colin took Noelle's hand in his and waited for her to tell George. She inhaled a deep breath.

"Although I've always planned to open my grandparents' summer camp and run it, I had another reason for coming here at this time. I wanted to meet you."

The older man gazed at her with a puzzled frown. "Why?"

"It's a long story. You see, my parents had tried to conceive for several years, but were unable to. My father's sperm count was too low. So finally they decided to try artificial insemination. My mother didn't want the sperm of a stranger, so since she knew Mackenzie and he was nearby in school, she asked him to be her sperm donor."

"Sperm donor?"

"Yes. Mackenzie is my donor father."

"Mackenzie was your daddy?"

"No. Mackenzie was my donor father. Franklin Greenwood is my father. He raised me and loved me. He's a good father."

"Mackenzie's wife couldn't have children." He peered at her closely. "You have his eyes."

She regarded Colin before she focused on the older man. "So I've been told."

"He knew you were his child. I'm sure that's why he spent so much time with you at the camp and brought you here during the summers."

"I guess so. I didn't know at that time. I only found out a year ago."

"And in all those years, you never saw each other. That must have been difficult for him."

George watched Noelle closely. Silence crackled in the room.

"You're my granddaughter. I have a granddaughter," he said softly. "I can't believe it. I thought…I thought…" He grappled with his words, as if he could barely believe what was happening.

Noelle reached out and touched his hand, and his fingers closed tightly around hers.

He cleared his throat. "You'll stay to dinner. There's plenty of food. Leila always cooks too much. You'd think she was feeding a family of ten."

"Maybe some other time. I'm afraid the roads will freeze when the temperature drops. I think I should get home."

"Spend the night here. Another storm's coming in tonight. What if the lights go out and you're all alone in that old house."

"I'll be fine. Besides, I didn't bring any clothes."

"Colin can go get some for you. I'll worry if you're there all alone. Spend the night," he repeated. He glanced at Colin. "Get a move on, son. If you're late to dinner, Leila won't like it."

"But—" she started.

"Dinner's in an hour."

"But—"

"Come on," Colin said, urging her out of the seat. "Tell me what I should bring back with me."

"I can't spend the night," she whispered once they were in the hallway.

"I've seen more life in him tonight than I've seen in months. Just humor him, okay? It's just for one night. You can give him that much."

"Okay, but I'm going back with you."

Outside, the roads were already beginning to freeze, but Colin had no trouble negotiating them.

"Pack enough for a couple of days at least," Colin called out when she went upstairs. "And don't forget your bathing suit."

Noelle smiled with hope as she added the suit to her overnight case. She'd need her hair dryer and shampoo if she used the pool. A simple sleepover was turning into an adventure.

"I can't stay that long." But she packed enough for three days.

When they returned, Leila was setting the dining-room table with the best china and linens.

"Why he wants fine china for chili is beyond me. But I'm just the hired help," Leila mumbled.

"You act as if you own the place," Colin said.

"Who asked you?" Leila snapped back.

"May I help?" Noelle asked.

"George is waiting for you in the sitting room. Better not keep him waiting. He's been waiting on pins and needles for y'all to get back, as if Colin suddenly forgot how to drive." The older woman shook her head.

With the fine china in the formal dining room Noelle felt underdressed.

"I should have brought something nicer to wear for meals."

"We never dress here."

"But still…"

"Don't worry about it. It's you he wants to see, not your clothes."

She reached for Colin's hand. "Thank you for helping me through this." She knew she'd lost him when he stiffened and pulled his hand from hers.

"George is improving already. This is for him."

George was indeed waiting for them. "I'll show you to your room and then you can join me in here," he said, leading the way.

They climbed the stairs to the second floor, and he led her to a huge bedroom suite decorated in blue and rose.

"I had Leila fix a little hot toddy for us. Always good on a cold snowy night."

She thanked him.

"Join us soon," he said.

Noelle quickly changed clothes and freshened up. When she went back down to the sitting room George and Colin were waiting for her. Colin, she noticed hadn't bothered to change. Obviously this wasn't a very special occasion for him.

"I brought down some of the family albums. Mostly the ones with pictures of Mackenzie. There are pictures of his mother, too. I'll have to take you by his practice as soon as the snow clears some."

"I'd like that." He was clearly eager to share his son with her.

"Colin and I will show you around the farm," he said.

"I've seen quite a bit of it already. It's impressive."

"It's part of your heritage. You need to know about thoroughbred horses."

"Mr. Avery, I'm not here to get involved with your farm. I just wanted to meet you. I wanted to learn more about my donor father."

He smiled brightly. "And I want to know everything about you."

* * *

The dinner of chili and cornbread was delicious. Leila was still puzzled about the special occasion until George informed her that Mackenzie was Noelle's father. He totally ignored the donor part.

"I knew there was something special about her," she said. "I always knew it."

"Why?" George asked.

"Because he was so taken with the child. I remember how he'd have her over here during the summers every chance he got. He was so patient with her. And you're like him, Noelle. I think I'm just going to cry. So when are you moving in?"

"I'm not," Noelle said.

"But this is a big house. No sense in you being over there alone."

"I like my grandparents' house."

"It's nice but...George?"

"We'll discuss it later," he said.

The last thing she needed was for Colin's words to seem true. If she moved in, he'd think she was like William, that she was after what she could get. And she couldn't bear that.

Colin had to get out of there or bust. After dinner, he excused himself from drinks in the sitting room and drove to the barns. His trainer was watching the closed-circuit TV so he could observe a pregnant mare without disturbing her.

"Looks like she's going to drop tonight," he said.

Colin regarded the monitor. "Has her water broken yet?"

"Not yet."

The mare was in the birthing barn, which had a special large stall that was round instead of rectangular. The floor was covered with a deep bed of straw.

The mare was restless. This was to be one of Diamond Spirit's foals, and they had great plans for its future.

"I better give George a call," the trainer said. "He wanted to bring someone down to see the birthing."

Colin stifled a curse. He'd wanted to get away from Noelle.

Colin couldn't have made it more evident that he wanted nothing to do with her, Noelle thought, pain slicing through her. She and George sat in the den talking. The curtains were open and with the light outside they watched the snow drift slowly to the ground.

George questioned her about her high-school

and college years. What her favorite classes had been. What extracurricular activities she'd participated in. Her boyfriends. George wanted to know everything. If she mentioned something Mackenzie also did, he pointed it out to her.

Finally the phone rang and George answered it. The conversation was short.

"A foal is going to be born tonight. Why don't we change clothes and go to the barn," George said. "I had Leila put out an old coat and some jeans for you. Have you ever seen a foaling?"

"No."

"Then you're in for an experience."

Noelle quickly changed and George drove them to the barn. She saw Colin's truck parked outside, and her stomach muscles clenched. When they went inside he and another man were watching the monitor.

"How's it going, Burt?" George asked.

"She's coming along."

"Have you met Noelle?"

"Haven't had the pleasure, sir." The man stood and came to shake her hand. "Pleased to meet you, ma'am." Then he turned to George. "The vet's on the way," he said. "He'll probably spend the night. Getting slippery out there."

George nodded.

From the monitor Noelle noticed the mare kept staring at her belly and becoming more restless.

Burt left the room to check on her. When he came back, he said, "Her water broke. Shouldn't be long now."

Colin and Burt left the observation area and went into the stall. Minutes later, the vet came in.

"How's it going?" he asked. "Sure could use some coffee. Busy night."

After George introduced Noelle, she offered to get the coffee. "What would you like in it?"

"Just plain."

"Let me show you where the pot is," George said, leading the way to another room with a table and small appliances. Hot coffee was already made, so Noelle filled a clean cup, taking it to the vet.

With long gloves on his arms that extended all the way up to his shoulders, he was examining the mare. When he finished he peeled the gloves off and came for his coffee. But after he'd taken only a couple of sips, a whitish sack appeared from the mare.

"There she goes," Burt said.

Soon after, a couple of feet appeared, then the head. The sac broke and the mare continued to move around.

"She keeps getting up and lying down to ensure the foal is kept in the right position," George said.

Then the mare seemed to rest.

Colin seemed so totally absorbed. He was clearly enjoying the arrival of a new thoroughbred.

And then the foal was delivered. The air was brimming with excitement.

"Welcome to the world, little guy," the vet said.

Colin's gaze met hers. His eyes were warm and hopeful. For a second they were a couple again and her first instinct was to grab and hug him, but then his smile subsided and he turned his attention to the foal who managed to stand on pencil-thin, wobbly legs.

"The legs are so long in comparison with his body," Noelle said to George, who came up beside her.

"He'll be that way for a while." Noelle had never seen George's smile so wide.

The next morning, Colin rose early and, even before Leila prepared coffee, he went outside. He was happy George had Noelle, but he didn't need the constant reminder of what a big fool he'd made of himself.

The storm had finally cleared out, leaving

behind six inches of snow, untouched except for a small animal's pawprints leading into the distant woods. With the mountains looming in the background and snow covering trees, bushes and buildings, the farm looked like a fantasy wonderland. What a great day to walk through the snow or have a snowball fight, he thought.

Retrieving the shovel, he cleared the steps and sidewalk before he maneuvered the truck through the snow to the office. Fair weather or foul, the animals had to be cared for. Soon, one of the stable hands would get out the snowplow and clear the driveways and path to the stables.

In the office, he turned up the temperature gauge and made coffee. Then he went into the stable and looked over the horses.

An hour later, he was at his desk when he heard a truck drive up. George was at the wheel, but Noelle got out carrying a small basket in her hand. Her face was flushed by the time she made it into the building.

"Leila sent breakfast," she said, setting the basket on his desk. At that moment, his stomach reminded him of how hungry he was.

"It's a huge breakfast," she said. "She packed enough for two people. I think I gained a couple of pounds off what I ate."

"I doubt that," Colin said.

Usually he would give her one of those looks, but not this time. He merely thanked her for the basket and started to take the contents out.

For the first time, Noelle felt awkward in his presence. She cleared her throat. "Colin?"

George walked in, stomping his boots on the mat. "Wicked cold out there. You're about early. Think I'll show Noelle the barns and spend a little time in the office," he said.

"After the tour, I'll go back home," Noelle said to Colin. "Can you take me, or shall I get someone else?"

"The snow's too deep to drive the roads," George piped in. "Too dangerous. Crazy drivers out there."

And because he seemed so worried, Noelle decided not to push it. She'd brought enough clothing to last a couple of days anyway. She gave Colin an assessing glance before she left with George.

"You know, my grandfather started this farm, buying up small parcels at a time until it grew," George told her as they walked to the barns. "Colin's grandfather bought a portion of the estate when things were lean. We attended college together. His grandfather started a business in D.C. that did very well, and when he retired, he turned it over to his children. Colin's father runs the business now. He never approved of his father's purchase or took any interest in the farm. Thought it was a waste of money."

"It's beautiful. This place is larger than I thought."

"Colin loves it. He's the only grandchild who does. His father sometimes entertains business associates in the summerhouse. It's on another portion of the property that's not as secure as the stables."

By the time they made it through the barns, Colin had come outside. He stood for a moment and gazed at the horizon while he pulled on his gloves, then he headed to the barn with lean grace and purpose. He belonged here, she thought.

Desire, sharp and painful, swept through her. She should have done things differently. She should have told him who she was from the very beginning, but she couldn't turn back the clock. She'd made a mistake, and he'd decided not to forgive her. There wasn't a thing she could do about it.

Chapter 10

Colin didn't see Noelle again until dinnertime. When he'd come in from work he'd heard her and George talking in the den. Ignoring them, he'd gone to his room and called Simone. Maybe she wasn't his girlfriend, but she was someone he'd dated off and on. He wasn't going to stare at the ceiling and dream half the night about Noelle. Enough was enough. Women were women after all, easily replaceable.

He'd showered and donned fresh clothes before he came downstairs. The smell of hot apple cider drew him toward the den.

"Would you like something stronger in yours?" George asked as he poured him a cup.

"Please," Colin said, knowing very well that George would spike it with rum. Then he got his first glimpse of Noelle. She looked beautiful in a lavender angora sweater and tight-fitting jeans. Heat ripped through his body.

He was glad he'd made the date. Simone wasn't complicated. She was a career woman and didn't want a man cramping her style. He wasn't ready for love ever after, either.

"I was thinking that after dinner, you and Noelle—" George started.

"I've got plans," Colin cut in.

"But the roads—"

"My four-wheel drive can handle it," he said. That excuse about the roads might keep the green Noelle stranded there, but not him. He knew they'd already been plowed and salted.

He hated the disappointed look on George's face. The older man would see a match with Noelle as one made in heaven. Their unity would combine the property.

But Colin didn't trust Noelle any longer. For George's sake, he contained his anger.

* * *

Colin forced himself through an uncomfortable dinner. He could feel Noelle's eyes on him. She looked as if she didn't understand what she'd done, why he was cooling it between them. George watched him, too, and when he did, Colin tried to show how pleased he was the two of them were together.

He was glad when dinner was finally over and he could leave Noelle with George showing her pictures and telling her stories of Mackenzie.

At the last minute Colin added a touch of cologne. He really didn't like the stuff but Simone did. He had to get Noelle out of his head and Simone was just the woman to do it. She was one gorgeous woman with curves in all the right places. Her face was beautiful, if a little hardened by life. But women had to be strong these days. Hell, Noelle wasn't a cream puff by any stretch of the imagination.

At Simone's place Casey answered the door and called upstairs.

"Simone, your date's here." Then she glanced at Colin. "I can't believe you're cutting out on Noelle that way. George isn't going to like it."

"If my personal life is a problem for you, you can find a job elsewhere."

She pinched her lips. "You didn't hire me. George did. You're as mean as people are saying. I wish you'd make up with Noelle so you can become more human again. But since my opinion isn't appreciated…"

"It isn't."

"I'll just leave you alone then." She gathered freshly laundered clothes off the sofa and escaped upstairs.

Women, Colin thought. *Always trying to give advice.* Everyone was giving him advice about Noelle. Everyone loved her.

The other roommate came downstairs. "Can I get you something to drink?" she asked. "Simone had a late interview. She's still getting dressed."

"I'm fine." Colin sat on the couch and glanced around the small place Simone shared with the two other women. Hip-hop music was blasting from another room, and the sharp smell of Chinese food was prevalent. The room wasn't quite as neat as Noelle's place, but he didn't date Simone for her housekeeping skills.

He smiled. She had skills in another department.

Simone came downstairs wearing tight jeans

with a deep-V-neck blue sweater. She was hot and sexy as heck. Yeah. This is definitely what he needed to rid his dreams of Noelle. He'd sleep like a baby tonight.

"So where are we going?" Simone asked.

"I take it you've had dinner?"

"Yes. I'm watching my weight."

"What about a coffee house or a lounge?"

"What about your place?"

"Too crowded."

"Not the summerhouse. We can make a fire in the fireplace. Or we can go to your office. You have a nice couch there."

The image of him snuggled up with Noelle in the blanket in front of the fireplace came to mind, but he could make new memories to erase the old ones. "Wouldn't take long to get warm," he said. He also had a nice bottle of Scotch they could polish off.

Simone grabbed her coat and purse and they were driving to the summerhouse.

"I like a woman who knows what she wants."

The date was a disaster.

It was supposed to have been a great evening. Drinks in front of the fire with a beautiful woman.

Lovemaking so spectacular his memories of Noelle would fade to a blur.

It didn't work out that way. He'd made a fire in the summerhouse fireplace, all right, and even closed the doors to keep the heat in. It was soon as cozy and warm as they'd imagined. Colin grabbed a couple of blankets. He'd even poured the drinks and snuggled with Simone on the couch.

Only thing, he'd kept wishing he had Noelle in his arms. And every time he tried to kiss Simone, Noelle's face flashed across his vision. Noelle's soft lips forced him to pull back from Simone. Frustrated, he finally gave up, peeved with himself. He pulled back.

"What is it?" Simone asked, puzzled, reaching for him.

Colin swiped a hand across his face. "I'm sorry, Simone. Earlier, I thought this was a good idea."

"So, you had a fight with your girlfriend and thought a night with me would give you relief? Or maybe you took your fantasy far enough to think you'll get over her completely."

"She's not my girlfriend."

"You want her to be. Look, I don't have to be a genius to know that." She glared at him with disgust. "You know the main reason I don't take guys seriously is because you all can be so obtuse. You date women you don't give a damn about just because you're too dense to patch up whatever the heck is wrong with the one you want. Don't use me as a substitute again. I love good sex, but I don't like wasting my time. I'm too busy."

"Simone—"

"Go to a priest if you need to confess." She got her coat. "Take me home and patch it up with Noelle."

Simone hugged the door all the way back to her house. Silence screamed into the night. She had every right to be angry with him.

"Sorry about the evening," he said.

She grabbed the handle to her door. "Don't bother getting out. I can see myself in. You owe me a damn good interview."

Colin waited until she got in the house before he backed out of the drive. Then he laughed as he pulled off. Leave it to Simone not to let a good business opportunity go to waste.

On his way home, he passed Noelle's place. His gut tightened. This was worse than anything he could have imagined. He rarely gave women a second thought when the relationship was over. He took refuge in his work, but this time it was different.

Noelle had turned his world upside down and he hated it.

* * *

Noelle stayed two extra days. George took her home, helping her carry in two bar stools she'd bought on a shopping trip with him. He helped her unpack them in the kitchen and took the empty boxes with him when he left, after he shoveled the driveway and the steps.

He'd taken his duties as a grandfather seriously.

Before she made it upstairs, a real estate agent called. He had a client who wanted to make an offer on her property.

She'd already made it clear that her land wasn't for sale, but that didn't keep the vultures from circling. Her camp was prime acreage for development.

Quickly getting him off the phone, she turned her heat up a couple of degrees. Two minutes later, a car drove into the yard. Even though Noelle had given up on Colin changing his mind about them, hope still rose when she answered the door—not to Colin, but to Carp. She gave him a hopeful smile she just wasn't feeling.

"Some snow we had, wasn't it? The schools in Baltimore were closed. Gave me a chance to spend more time with my children."

"Well, judging by your smile, I don't need to ask how your weekend went, do I?"

"Couldn't be better."

"Don't just stand there. Come in and tell me all about it," she said.

"I'll take a few minutes," he said, glancing at his watch. Lately, he seemed to take pride in getting to work on time and doing a good job.

Noelle lead him to the kitchen and put on a pot of coffee while he shed his coat and sat on one of the new bar stools.

"I got to spend hours each day with them. The last night they stayed with me at the hotel. My son had a basketball game Friday night. He's quite the player," he said. "He's always loved sports. I was a little worried that he'd let sports take precedence over his schoolwork. You know how boys are. They all think they're going to be the next Michael Jordan. But he's got his head on straight," he said with a father's proud air. "My daughter's a cheerleader. She's a real beauty and smart." Carp shook his head. "You know you don't think kids are listening when you talk, but when I asked my son about his future he said, 'Dad, I remember what you said. I might get a scholarship, but I'm not counting on basketball as a career. I want to be an accountant. I know it's not the hip thing so I don't talk about it.'"

"You must be so proud."

"I am. My daughter wants to be a pediatrician." Carp leaned back with his chest out. "I've got to put something by to help them. If I have to work day and night, I'm going to see that they make it to college. My house is paid for. My brothers helped me build it. It's not much, but it's a roof over my head."

"It's more than just a roof over your head," Noelle assured him. "It's a cozy home most people would be proud to own."

"Nice of you to say," he said and shook his head. "Was a time a kid could be proud of going on to school and making something of himself. When did it get to the point our kids have to be ashamed of wanting to better themselves?"

"Indirectly they hear it all the time. There's the peer pressure. And I have nothing against preachers and the church. I'm not on the bashing bandwagon. Our religion centers us. As a matter of fact, I have to find a church here. But how many times have we heard we might have a degree and we might make money, but it won't get us to heaven?"

"A lot more than we hear beating your wife, selling dope to kids and not working to support your family is wrong, that's for sure."

"It sends mixed messages to our children."

"A man is supposed to work and take care of his family," Carp murmured, some of the euphoria leaving him. "If you're looking for a church, I'll be happy to give you the name of mine and introduce you to the minister. It's the same church George attends, although he hasn't been much since his son died."

"Maybe I'll get him to go with me."

"Good idea. I need to get over there and see how he's doing," Carp said, gathering his coat. "Well, have to get to work. Stop by later on if you have the time."

At least someone's life was going in the right direction, Noelle thought, pleased for Carp as she saw him out. He looked like a different man from the downtrodden one of the month before.

Weeks passed and though Noelle hoped the warm feelings that had passed between Colin and her after the foal's birth would at least get him to see reason, the camaraderie had been short-lived. Colin had gone back to his old keep-his-distance self.

It was February and breeding season had begun on the farm. She saw Colin several times a week and as much as she caught him sneaking glances at her, he treated her like a friend's daughter, not as his previous lover. At least George was improving daily. Unfortunately her feelings for Colin hadn't abated at all.

Noelle was working in her office one morning; she'd just received the brochures that she'd ordered for the campground. Already she'd placed ads in magazines in the D.C. metro area as well as Maryland and Philly. Brent had sponsored ten students from Memphis. He'd convinced some of his contemporaries to sponsor slots, as well. So far, places for fifty children had been filled on his recommendation alone. The company that was donating the computers had purchased space for five students.

She'd also mailed out help-wanted notices to college campuses to fill the counselor slots for the summer. The computer and investment teachers had already been hired.

Carp had completed the work on the girls' dorm and was now working on the boys'. He expected to be completely finished by the middle of May. The grounds crew would begin work in early March.

Noelle went to the kitchen to make coffee and heard a car approach. Probably Carp, she thought and was glad she'd made extra coffee. But she answered the door to George—and a dog.

"Brought you a little present." The gift was straining at the leash, hopping around and sniffing. "Don't like you being out here alone. Since you won't stay with me, I have some protection for you."

"How nice," she said with less enthusiasm than either George or the dog were displaying.

"Nice little guy," George said. "Lets you know if somebody's snooping around. Will protect you, too."

"If you say so," Noelle muttered, although the dog wasn't little at all. "Where am I supposed to keep it?"

"Wherever you want to. She's used to being indoors."

"I've never had a dog before," she said skeptically. "They seem to be a lot of work."

"Not half as much as horses."

"Have to keep things in perspective," Noelle murmured.

"Her name's Trixie. I have some food for her to get you started. She's up to date on her shots. How is work coming on the camp?"

He was in such a jovial mood she hated to bust his bubble, but a dog?

"Very good. Have a seat and drink some coffee while I get you a brochure." Noelle poured a cup for him before she went to the office to retrieve a brochure.

George had used some excuse to stop by nearly every day. He'd given her some of his wife's old jewelry, doling it out one piece at a time. Each piece had a story attached to it. At first she'd refused to accept the gifts, but he seemed so disappointed that she'd accepted some of them. She'd told him over and over he didn't need to bring gifts to stop by. She was always pleased to see him, but he wasn't listening.

They'd gone to church together a couple of Sundays, although he still refused to attend grief sessions. Now a dog. Noelle closed her eyes briefly. What in the world was she going to do with a dog?

Things had definitely been looking up, Colin thought. Any day now, one of their most promising mares would give birth, netting them enough to pay off a major loan and bringing them into the black for the first time in years. Then he could get his dad off his back.

As much as Noelle was stealing his sleep, he realized one thing: he'd work with her any day before he worked for William. At least she cared about George and the farm.

An hour later, Colin got the fateful call.

The foal had been stillborn. Colin could hardly believe it. Like a gambler he'd counted on the foal pulling them out of debt. It wasn't the only foal due, but the money for the others was already spoken for. There was the feeding and care of the animals, including vet services. Payroll was high and couldn't be cut. Then there were the fees for transporting the horses and entering races. Everything cost loads of money.

He felt like a gambler who'd bet his last dollar and lost. He was tired of scrimping and barely getting by. Hard work didn't faze him, but he was tired of arguing with his dad over why the farm should survive.

One little break. That was all he'd needed. One freaking break. For the rest of the day he worked his frustrations off in the barn. Hours later he was bone-tired when he left for the house.

When Colin came in from the barn, his brothers were in the kitchen regaling Leila with some tales that had the woman laughing so hard tears ran down her cheeks.

"What're you doing here?" Colin asked, not in the mood to entertain.

Aaron, his older brother, held up the deck of cards. "Blake's here, too, talking to George somewhere." Blake was their cousin. "Thought we'd break the boredom out here. See if we can pick your pockets."

"You wish you could be so lucky. Give me a half hour."

"Takes you that long to get prettied up now?" Michael, the youngest, muttered.

"Heard he has a new girlfriend. All that dating must have him tired out."

"She's a nice girl," Leila said, always quick to defend him.

"So when do we meet her?" Aaron asked.

"You don't," Colin said and left. Noelle was the last person he wanted to think about, but he knew his brothers weren't going to let him drop the topic. He quickly showered.

By the time he made it back, Leila had a spread of food on the table. His brothers had contributed bottles of liquor and cigars to the poker game. Although he ate, he drank more. He should have known better.

He lost.

Everyone except his oldest brother went to bed around two.

"I think I'll head in," Colin said.

"Want to talk about it?"

"How did you hear so fast?"

"The old man."

"Figures. He'll want to sell for sure now."

"Don't let him. Colin, you love this place. He's running through a rough patch at the office, but we'll pull through. It's not about you anyway. Dad's got issues with Grandpa he never resolved. Don't let him lay that burden on you," Aaron said. "Anybody who'd take the time to notice can appreciate what you're doing here. Grandpa would be proud. You know he started the company in D.C. to support his family, but he bought into this place because he loved it. So you hang in there. Do what you have to do to hold on to this place."

Colin shook his head, feeing just a little better. "You've always been in my corner."

"We're family. So when am I going to meet this Noelle Dad keeps talking about?"

George was in the office bright and early Monday morning. "That you, Colin? I want to talk to you."

Colin poured himself a cup of coffee and joined George. He was very pleased with the man's improvement the last few weeks. "What's up?"

"I'm sending out invitations for a party the last of the month to introduce Noelle to the family. I'll make the announcement at the party."

"Sounds good."

"I'm also changing my will. I'm leaving the farm to Noelle. She doesn't know it yet. I'm thinking that eventually you'll get the other half and the two of you can work together. I know she's set on opening that camp, but once the buildings are repaired, she'll have more time on her hands. The camp only runs in the summer. She has to do something the rest of the year. She can work on the farm. The two of you can work together, can't you? Starting in September after camp is closed, I'd like you to help familiarize her with the workings of the farm."

"Be glad to," Colin said, feeling anything but glad.

"I'll send out the invitations this week. Won't the family be surprised?"

What an understatement, Colin thought.

"For a time I thought you and Noelle would get on. Be a good match."

Colin tucked his hands in his pockets. Time wasn't healing his ache for her. "I don't know, George."

"It's time you settled down. I wouldn't want you settling with her if you aren't sure. But you'd sure make a good husband if you set your mind to it. You're more like your grandfather than you think. He ran around like crazy until your grandmother came along." George laughed. "He'd never admit it to family, but he was quite the hound in his day. But once Marlene caught his eye, well, he never cheated on her. I'm thinking you're just like him. You seemed to like her."

This wasn't a subject Colin wanted to explore with George. "She's a nice lady. And I'm happy for you. But we'll see where this leads."

Disappointed, the older man nodded and Colin left for his office.

The next day William's truck jerked to a stop in front of the office. He hopped out without his jacket, and marched toward the building.

Colin had been watching Noelle with a foal. He took a moment to admire her backside before he headed to the office, too. As soon as he entered the warm reception area he shucked his jacket and hung it on the coat tree. William's raised voice was all he heard.

"What's going on, Uncle George? Mama told me you had your will changed."

"That's right," George's voice said strong and clearer than anything Colin had heard for a while. "But I'm going to have to talk to the lawyer. He had no business discussing that with anyone."

"She doesn't know what was changed, but why change it at all? Look, Uncle George, this isn't the time to make drastic changes. I keep telling you to spend some time with us. I think you need some help. It's dangerous making a move like that out of the blue in your frame of mind. This is a wonderful farm. I know the vultures are circling, but you need to make sure that it's in the possession of someone who can handle things if for any reason you can't. I feel you have many good years ahead of you. But life has a way of shocking us."

"I know that better than anyone," George said. "Trust me. It's in good hands. Now, we won't discuss this anymore. I've already changed my will and I'll stand by my decision. Although I appreciate your concern and the fact that you visit me to make sure I'm doing well." George smiled. "But it's my will and really none of your business."

Colin stood leaning against the doorjamb watching the show. Colin was sure William was gritting the enamel off his teeth. The man couldn't afford to make a move that would alienate George.

"Now, why don't you have lunch with us?" George asked. "Can you join us, Colin?"

"I've already eaten."

William swiveled quickly, unaware Colin was behind him. He narrowed his eyes at Colin before he focused on George. "Wish I could stay, but I need to get back. I have a meeting in an hour and my desk is overflowing."

"Thanks for stopping by," George said. "And try to get your mother to stay a week or so while she's here."

"The weather is unpredictable this time of year, and she doesn't like to drive if snow's on the ground," William said.

Colin left for his office and smiled. George was more his old cunning self again. He'd learned much from the wily old man. Colin left his door open so he could continue to eavesdrop on the conversation.

"I'll do my best to get her to stay," William said, but he didn't leave. He stood in the reception area and watched George leave, then he went to Colin's office and closed the door.

William starting pacing in front of the window watching George and Noelle climb into his truck and leave.

"Colin, do you know what's going on?"

"Sure," he said. "I run this place. Why don't you have a seat?" Comfortable, Colin leaned back in his chair.

But William didn't sit; he continued to pace across the carpet. "Well?"

"If you have concerns you need to talk to George. It's not my place to carry messages. You're family, after all."

William's face froze to stone. "I can't wait to get my hands on this place," he said. "There's so much that can be done with it."

"I'm sure you can't, but don't make plans prematurely."

William regarded him suspiciously. "Mama told me Uncle George is planning a party. What's this business about a party in the middle of the winter? He never gives parties, and especially not this time of year."

"Didn't you talk to George about it?"

"You know very well he's being secretive."

"You'll have to attend the party next weekend to find out."

"I want to know what's going on. Now."

"Then talk to George," Colin said, knowing very well he wouldn't.

Furious, William stomped off.

Yes, indeed, Colin thought. *You should worry. Because the little windfall you thought you were getting isn't coming your way.*

Colin returned to the barn. They had a couple of mares to cover that day. Many owners wanted their mares mounted so the foals would be born as close as possible to the beginning of the next year.

Now that they weren't getting the money expected from the stillborn foal, the extra coming in for breeding would at least keep the bills paid.

Colin had just enough time for a quick shower before dinner, but when he drove to the house, he spotted his father's car before he saw Noelle's. He wasn't in the mood to deal with his dad. Sighing, he left his truck and went straight to his suite. He at least needed a shower and a chance to clear his head before he faced the old man.

Twenty minutes later Colin descended the stairs. Everyone was in the den munching on appetizers Leila had served. He poured himself a shot of Scotch.

Colin looked as if he'd aged, Noelle thought. She hoped it wasn't because of her. He seemed to be sleeping as well as she was—which was very little.

He was driving himself needlessly. She'd tried to console him over the weekend when she heard about the foal, and his reception had seemed warmer than usual.

"I was just telling your father what a help you are to Noelle in training her in the business," George said.

Colin threw Noelle a glance before he focused on George.

"As well he should since they're dating," his father said.

Colin started to speak, but George cut him off.

"Needless to say, I'm very pleased with the match," George said. "You'll be the first to know, Leander, that Noelle is Mackenzie's daughter. And of course I've already changed my will. She'll be getting my portion of the farm. I couldn't hope for a more perfect match personally or business-wise."

"Your granddaughter?" Leander said.

"It's a long story. I'll be introducing her to the family next weekend. I hope you can attend the party."

Noelle felt like a costumed doll on display. She really didn't want the farm. That's all Colin needed to prove his point—that she was only after George's money. But she knew if William got it, he'd sell it out of hand. George had worked too hard to let that happen. And so had Colin. George and Colin's grandfather believed in it. Colin could run the farm when the time came. And perhaps she could help.

"Maybe the boy's finally growing up," Leander said. "I can't tell you how pleased I am that Colin has finally settled down with a nice young lady. A good woman can take the wanderlust out of a man, you know."

The right blood lines, Colin thought. Would his father never understand? Losing the foal was all the excuse his father needed to convince himself he needed to sell his portion of the thoroughbred farm. Colin would need some of the cunning he'd learned from George to pull this one off.

Chapter 11

"Heard you lost the foal."

The voice was like a knife twisting in his gut. Colin didn't have to turn around to identify his father's voice. He knew he'd have to face the music, though he'd hoped to avoid it now, having escaped to the stable after dinner.

Steeling his emotions, he faced the older man. His father wasn't alone. The man who'd wanted to buy River Oaks for the last year was with him. He must have arrived while Colin was at the stable.

Colin's stomach roiled. His father got the trainer to show the buyer around. When they were alone,

Colin pulled his father aside. It ticked him off that his father was so willing to give up. But he reined in his emotions to deal with the situation logically.

"Dad, there are always going to be setbacks. That doesn't mean we have to give up the business."

"That's exactly my point. You're never going to be able to hold your head above water. This is a risky business. It takes a lot of money. And I don't want you to live your life that way."

"For once we have a stallion whose offspring are winning races. We're getting decent rates for stud fees off this stallion alone. This year we'll bring in at least five million, if not more."

"You're still teetering on the edge. This kind of business can drain you dry. It will always be this way."

"But the rewards are worth it. The business has been pulling itself up in the last couple of years. Granddad and George laid the groundwork. They weren't going by trial and error. They had a plan and now we're executing it. And it's working. If you just give me a year we'll be in the black."

"You thought you'd be in the black with this foal. But look what happened. Son, you'll say the same thing six months from now. A year from now. Two years from now."

Colin inhaled sharply. There was only one way to settle this. "Dad, let me buy you out."

His father barked out a laugh. "With what? You don't have two nickels to rub together."

"I have some savings and I have all the money Granddad left me. I haven't spent a penny of it. Write up a contract. The same one the other buyer will offer you. I'll make the first payment in six months."

"I'm not going to let you ruin your life that way. I'm not going to let what happened to Dad happen to you."

"Why do you keep saying that? Nothing happened to Granddad. He bought into a business, set up a plan and now it's working," Colin said. "Every sales venture you make at your company doesn't pan out. You've had losses, but you don't sell the business because of them. You keep trying. This is no different. It's a business with ups and downs just like the one you run."

His father wasn't hearing him. He was still shaking his head.

"Can't you see that Grandpa was happy? Do you hate your job so much you can't stand to see me enjoy my work? Let me choose my career."

"You enjoy the celebrity, Colin. You enjoy the women. You stand out in this business just like any athlete," he said. "You can work at the company. Then maybe you can start to settle down. How's the new girlfriend by the way?"

"Dad, did you hate Grandpa? What did he do to you?"

"What the heck is this about?" Leander asked.

"I don't think your issues with the farm are about me. There's more going on here."

"It has nothing to do with your grandfather."

"Then why do you treat me differently from my brothers? They aren't perfect. They date as many women as I have, yet you don't hold it over their heads. You don't even concern yourself with it. And you don't threaten to fire them every time they do something wrong at the company. You're not being fair. So I want to know why. What have I done that's so bad compared to them?"

"I'm not threatening you. I'm looking out for your future."

"That's not true and you know it."

The buyer came out of the stable and his father started to walk away.

"Write up a contract," Colin said. "I'm offering to buy you out. Then, whether I win or lose, I'm in a place where I can make decisions I can live with."

Colin turned from his father and stalked away. He

went directly to Diamond Spirit's stall and fed him an apple. It took awhile for him to calm down, but watching the horse had a tendency to soothe him.

He thought of Noelle. He'd set her up to conform to some impossible standard, the same as his father was doing to him. Why hadn't he seen it before now? His love for her hadn't dissipated, not one bit. And he'd treated her unfairly. By now she'd probably sock him if he approached her. It would be nothing more than he deserved.

Noelle spent some time drinking a cup of apple cider and talking with Leila. Colin still hadn't come to the house. Leander and George were at the barns. The buyer had left half an hour ago.

"I tell you it just pains me," Leila said. "The boy works so hard. He loves this place every bit as much as his grandfather did. I just wish he could catch a break."

"So do I," Noelle said.

"You care about this place. You don't know squat about horses, but it doesn't matter. It's in your blood," she said.

"If you say so."

"I do. Colin ran around here wild as could be for years, but he was always good with the horses, even when he was a young one. As much as his father complained, his grandfather was patient. Said the boy would find his way eventually. And, of course, he did." She put together the fixings for a casserole for the next day. "Then it was the women. Colin was like a starving man with a feast. Didn't know which one to choose. They all looked good to him. And I told his grandfather that one day he was going to find one woman who'd tie him into knots until he wouldn't know which way was up."

"Oh, yeah?"

"His grandfather said he couldn't wait for that day."

"I think you were wrong."

"I wasn't wrong. So when are you going to put him out of his misery?"

On a morning later that week, Noelle was working in her office—at least she was trying to work when she wasn't thinking about the mess she'd made of things—when Trixie started yapping beside her. She pranced back and forth to the door. Noelle had gotten somewhat used to the creature. She'd fixed up a soft pallet beside her desk. The dog liked being near her for some odd reason. At night she slept beside the bed, now that Noelle had trained her not to sleep on the bed or on her furniture. Noelle was scared to death she'd step on her one night on her way to the bathroom, but Trixie wouldn't sleep in another spot.

Seconds later, she heard a car door slam. "Now I know what the prancing was about," she said as she went to the front door to answer it. "Soon I'll know all your little quirks." But before she twisted the lock, a hard pounding shook the door and nearly scared the daylights out of her. Her heart thumped as though it had been jump-started with a defibrillator.

"Open up!" a male voice thundered. "I know what you and Colin are up to. You've cooked up some scheme and I'm going to put an end to it." A fist rattled the door again. "You're not going to get away with it."

What in the world? "Go away," Noelle called out.

"I'm not leaving until you open that door."

Was he out of his mind? She wasn't about to open the door.

"Fine, then maybe the police will take you away."

"Open up!"

Noelle was actually trembling. *Who was out there?*

Trixie danced, barked and clawed at the door

as if she couldn't wait to take a bite out of whoever was on the other side. Noelle eased over to peer out of the side window, but she couldn't see the door.

The fist rattled her door again. She rushed to the phone and started to dial 911. Then she remembered he'd mentioned Colin.

Noelle didn't know what the lunatic was talking about, but she dialed Colin's cell number instead. The person obviously knew of him and of her. With an impatient voice, Colin answered immediately.

"Someone's banging on my door as if they're about to break in, yelling about a scheme we've worked up," she rushed out. "I'm about to call the police."

"I'll be right over," Colin said. She could barely hear his voice over the dog's barking. "Don't hang up," he cautioned. "Stay on the line with me."

"Okay," she murmured nervously, glancing at the rattling door. She was glad to have contact with someone sane. Her hand was trembling. Her stomach was jumping. The door was going to crash in any minute now. Noelle was never so happy to have an animal in her life. It occurred to her that she should get some other protection. There was a bat in the hall closet. Colin's voice was droning in the background, but with the dog's barking, she couldn't decipher his words.

Pulling on the dog's collar, she dragged her with her to the closet and retrieved the bat. Between the dog and the bat she should be okay until Colin arrived.

"The police are on the way. You'd better leave right now," Noelle yelled out, hoping her voice projected over the dog's barking.

"I'll be happy to tell them about your scheme and the two of you will go to jail just like you should. Open the damn door."

"Leave my house immediately. You're trespassing and you're crazy. I don't know about any scheme."

"Lady, you're hip-deep in it. I'll find out who you really are if it's the last thing I do."

The dog started tugging at the leash again, frantic to get to the intruder. Noelle didn't try to silence her.

"If you come in here, my dog will tear you to shreds." Thank God George had brought her the dog.

"Do you think I'm going to let a stupid mutt keep me away? I'm going to get the truth out of you. Who are you, some actress Colin hired? Or some cheap floozy he picked up somewhere?"

Finally Noelle gave up. Trixie was so worked up she could barely hear the man anyway. And since he wasn't trying to break the door down anymore, she could wait. But the trembling wracking her body wouldn't stop.

Finally she saw another truck drive into the yard and a couple more behind it, all with River Oaks Thoroughbred Farm emblazoned on the sides.

She could barely hear the vehicle doors slam over the din. Then she heard voices. The other trucks drove off. Only Colin and the intruder were left on the front porch. Obviously he knew the man.

Noelle grabbed the dog's collar and gingerly opened the door. She recognized George's nephew immediately. He was her cousin somewhere down the line, she realized.

"You!" William spat the words like bullets and glared at her. "He brought you here, didn't he? You're not Mackenzie's daughter. If he could have had children, his wife would have conceived years ago. They tried hard enough."

Colin stepped between them. "Noelle is George's granddaughter and there isn't a damn thing you can do about it. Get the hell out of here. Who do you think you are coming over here like this? If you have issues, take them up with George."

"You've got Uncle George wrapped around your fingers," William shouted at Noelle.

"It's not your business," Colin barked. "Now get out of here. And don't ever come back."

William pointed a shaky finger in Noelle's direction. "He changed the will because of you."

Noelle moved around Colin to face William. Now that she knew who he was, she wasn't hiding. "I don't need the farm. But you'd destroy everything George has built. I'll make sure that doesn't happen."

"You're getting everything when you don't deserve a damn thing. You won't get away with this. You watch and see." Although it was February and below freezing, William was sweating.

"It's all about the money with you, isn't it?" Colin sneered. "What you can get out of him. You don't give a crap about George. So take your deranged self away from here, because the deed's done and you can't do shit about it."

They watched William stomp to his car and drive off. Noelle rubbed Trixie's fur. The dog had finally stopped barking and sniffed Colin. He reached down and stroked her.

"You okay?" Colin asked Noelle.

She nodded.

"It's freezing. Let's go inside."

Trixie clearly wanted to stay outside, but Noelle feared if she let her out now, she'd follow William's car to the road and get hit.

"Thanks for coming over," Noelle said. She pressed a hand to her chest. The adrenaline was still flowing and she couldn't calm herself.

"I don't think he'll be back. He'll be too busy checking out your background."

"I'm surprised you didn't," Noelle said.

"How do you know I didn't?"

"I don't." Noelle wished he'd just leave. It was obvious he wanted nothing more to do with her, and try as she might, she couldn't banish him from her thoughts or her dreams. But the pain wouldn't last. She kept telling herself emotions had a way of healing. It was just happening too slowly to suit her. Or maybe she was giving up too quickly.

Women had always been easy for Colin. Maybe he didn't know what it took to work at keeping a relationship.

"Giving up is easy for you, isn't it?" Noelle said before she could stop herself. "You've chased women so long that you don't know how to fight for anything. You're running scared, aren't you? Because you put yourself on the line for this relationship. Women have just fallen at your feet in the past. You never cared about their feelings or about what they needed. It was all about you."

"They knew the score."

"Did I know the score? I love you. But it's my problem if you don't love me."

When he walked to the door, she thought he was going to leave without responding. Then taking his hand from the doorknob, he turned and faced her. "The funny thing is, I can't stop loving you—and believe me I've tried."

"I know you have." That fact saddened her. Two people who loved each other were separated because they couldn't find a way around their problems.

"We need to talk," Colin said. "But we can't right now. Diamond Spirit has to cover a mare soon," he said. "Come back to the farm with me."

"I don't—"

"George asked me to bring you," he said.

"I think you're using George as an excuse. He doesn't know you're here, does he? If he knew William was here, he'd have come with you."

Colin didn't acknowledge her one way or the other and Noelle knew he hadn't told George.

"I have to go, so could you please get your coat?" he asked.

"I was willing to trust what we shared even though I knew you'd probably break my heart. No. You aren't afraid of wild creatures or even some lunatic, but you're afraid of love, Colin Mayes."

"Can we talk about this later?"

She stared at him a long time, then she sighed. "I never would have kissed you if I hadn't had feelings for you. And I certainly never would have made love to you. Whether you believe me or not, my feelings were not lies. In the beginning I was afraid to trust you because of your reputation. You weren't exactly squeaky clean with women, but from the beginning, I thought you were truthful with me. That you were worth the risk. That you weren't lying. That you felt something for me, too."

Colin didn't know what to say. He needed time to deal with this, time he didn't have right then.

"So you're going to ignore me totally," he finally heard Noelle say. Deep in his own thoughts, he'd completely zoned her out.

"Get your coat, please," Colin finally said.

"Fine." She headed to the back of the house.

For the first time since his son's death, George entered Mackenzie's room. Dust covered every surface because he didn't allow Leila to clean it.

And since he was grieving so, she wouldn't fight him on it.

There were trophies and ribbons on the bookshelves. He touched them lovingly, remembering the time he'd spent at his son's games, and school and church plays. He was grateful that he'd participated in his son's life, that he hadn't let work interfere.

George picked up a photo of Mackenzie. There were many of him at different ages, and most of them were either on horseback or with horses.

Mackenzie was a large-animal vet. He'd enjoyed horses from the time he was no more than a young lad, when George would set him in front of him on the horse. George's wife—Mackenzie's mother—would come running out the door afraid the horse would rear up and tumble them both to the ground. But Mackenzie could never ride enough.

And then he saw pictures he'd never paid much attention to before. Pictures of Mackenzie and Noelle, taken when she'd spent summer vacations at her grandparents' home. Some were of her at summer camp when Mackenzie had taught her to ride. One was in Mackenzie's veterinary office. One was of her when she was older and riding a bicycle in a neighborhood of adobe houses and tropical plants. She looked unaware the picture was being taken.

George didn't realize that tears were running down his face until he felt the wetness on his cheeks. He swiped them away.

God had a way of working things out, he thought. If Mackenzie had asked his counsel on doing something as crazy as being a sperm donor, George would have argued with him day in and day out. But look at the precious gift he'd left his father. George smiled past the tears. Noelle looked just like a female Mackenzie. She was a beauty—and he wasn't prejudiced just because she was his granddaughter.

George spotted the register from Mackenzie's wake. Leila must have placed it there. Franklin and Harriet Greenwood's names and phone number were in there. He remembered they'd attended Mackenzie's funeral.

He'd jumped the gun, he realized suddenly. He should have spoken to Noelle's parents before he made plans for the party. It was never his intention to exclude or disrespect the couple who'd raised her, who were still the most important part of her. It was Mackenzie's decision to bow out of her existence after giving her life.

George sat on the bed and picked up the phone. It was seven in the morning in California. He dialed the Greenwoods' number, hoping they didn't leave early for work.

"I'm George Avery," he said when Franklin Greenwood responded. "It recently came to my attention that your daughter, Noelle, is my granddaughter. With your permission I want to announce her to my family. If you agree, I'd like to invite you to attend the party along with Gregory. He's a wonderful young man. I'm aware that both your parents are deceased, so I'm hoping you'll let me be a grandfather to her." He held his breath while he waited for the response. He knew Noelle was old enough to make her own decisions, but if he wanted a stress-free relationship with her, he had to get along with her family. George believed in family.

Franklin and George had a lengthy and pleasant conversation before Franklin said he would talk it over with his wife and call him that evening.

George knew he'd have to include Noelle's brother, too. He didn't want to create a division among siblings. And he remembered the two were close. He liked that. Many times he'd wished he'd given Mackenzie the siblings he'd wanted.

After hanging up the phone, George collected some of the pictures and placed a few in his room and more in the den downstairs.

"Leila!" he called out.

She came running out of the kitchen with a dish towel in her hand. "What is it?"

"Can you get one of the cleaning women to clean Mackenzie's room?"

Leila's just stared at him until she gained her composure. "I'll do it myself...right away."

George stifled a smile. She continued to stand as if rooted to the floor while she watched him don his coat and boots and leave the house. "I'll be back for lunch," he called over his shoulder. He frowned when he saw two of the farm trucks arriving filled with men. Why were they gallivanting about when they had a mare Diamond Spirit needed to cover?

Colin didn't want to think too much about his conversation with Noelle. The good thing about a thoroughbred farm was there was always enough work to keep his mind occupied. Right now he'd just gotten off the phone with the vet who had called to update Colin on the breeding session. He'd used a teaser horse to test the mare to see if she was ready for Diamond Spirit to mount her. When it was apparent the mare wasn't, he'd used the horse for foreplay.

Colin shut his phone and urged his truck faster

to the farm. He'd picked up Noelle, who sat beside him, asking questions about the breeding while absentmindedly petting the dog she'd insisted on bringing.

How was he going to make up for the way he'd treated her? He wanted to make things right, but it wasn't going to be easy. He smiled. At least she still loved him if he could believe that long speech she'd given.

He came to a halt at the house and hopped out, bringing the dog with him. The last thing he needed was that animal disturbing the horses. He ran into the house.

"Leila! Leila!"

"What is it?" she asked just before she appeared at the top of the stairs. "Everybody's screaming today."

"I'm leaving Noelle's dog with you."

"Not in this house, you're not."

"She's not coming with us to the breeding shed. I have to go," he said, leaving the dog in the foyer. As he left, he heard Leila muttering as she descended the stairs. That's what she got for talking George into getting the dog for Noelle in the first place, although, after William's escapade, Colin was glad for it.

By the time they drove to the shed, the men were

leading the teaser away. Colin walked up to the vet. "Is she ready?"

"Red-hot," the shorter man said. Colin introduced him to Noelle on the way into the shed.

She looked puzzled, seeing the mare's hind feet being covered with padded boots.

"The boots keep the mare from damaging Diamond Spirit if she kicks," Colin explained.

And then a handler led Diamond Spirit into the shed. He was frisky and seemed to know exactly why he was there. One of the workers held the mare's tail while Diamond Spirit approached the mare. When he covered her, the handler held her reins. A video camera recorded the session just in case the owner questioned them.

For Colin, it was pretty unnerving to be standing beside the woman who turned his guts inside out. Every sound and movement she made made him more aware of her, despite the seriousness of the action in the shed.

When Diamond Spirit dismounted the mare, the handler led her out.

Colin exited, too, leaving Noelle in George's capable hands.

He couldn't escape quickly enough, Noelle thought as she watched Colin leave the breeding shed.

"How's the latest foal?" she asked George.

"Good. Let's take a look." They started walking toward the barn.

The air was pungent with the smell of horse, manure and hay. The stablemen were mucking out some of the stalls.

The foal was nursing while the mother ate lunch.

"Is he too young to pet?" Noelle asked. The foal, with legs still too long in comparison with his body, looked cute.

"No. They have to get accustomed to human touch right away. He's one of Diamond Spirit's offspring. Frisky little fellow, isn't he?" George said.

"How many of Diamond Spirit's foals do you own?"

"Nine. I'd like to take you to races soon. One of Diamond Spirit's offspring is doing very well at the track."

Noelle smiled as she stroked the horse. "I'd like that."

Colin couldn't look too closely at the reason he'd told George about William's angry visit to Noelle's house. It certainly wasn't because he thought the nutcase would physically hurt Noelle. He was more talk than action. Besides, Colin believed William was too busy digging up information on Noelle and trying to disprove her connection to George to be a threat.

But Colin did know George would look for any excuse to spend more time with his granddaughter. So despite her stringent arguments, George had insisted she spend the night at the farm.

Colin should have known George would insist on going to town to confront William. Leila had quit muttering about the mutt long enough to go with him, probably afraid he'd keel over or something. She claimed she was saving her job. She had no intentions of working for William, she said, nor was she ready to retire just yet.

That left only him and Noelle at home—alone. When Colin came in, she was nowhere to be seen. He frowned as he searched the house. The dog was in the den on a rug near the fire.

He found Noelle in the whirlpool. She looked out of this world, wearing a skimpy two-piece, her breasts straining against the top. She sipped her drink, and, with her eyes closed, she leaned her head back. Her hair was wet. It was obvious she'd been swimming.

Desire hit him as hard as a kick from a horse. He stood there gazing at her for a full two minutes before he forced himself to look away and head up the stairs. In his room, he shucked his clothing and stood under the cool spray of the shower, trying to ease Noelle from his mind. But he couldn't erase the memory of her in the firelight weeks ago. He couldn't erase the one night they'd made love in her bed.

He couldn't erase his love for her.

He turned off the water and quickly dried off, then he donned his clothes and left his room. He was as hungry for Noelle as he was for food.

She was heading up the stairs with a towel wrapped around her as he started down. They were within inches of each other when she saw him. Her hair was wet and little rivulets of water dripped from the long stands.

Her eyes ran warily over him before she squared her chin. "Leila left your supper on the stove," she said.

"Got a minute?" Colin asked.

Puzzled, she answered him slowly, "Yes. What is it?"

"Let's go by the fire," he said. He wouldn't touch her, couldn't touch her if he were to hold on to his sanity, if he wanted to sound coherent.

Colin tried to figure out what to say. The one

thing women loved to hear was a man admitting he was wrong. Maybe he should just say it and get it over with.

She sat on the hassock near the fire, rubbing the water from her hair. She looked so good he wanted to rip the towel and the two scraps of bathing suit off her and make love with her until she screamed in pleasure. And the blazing fire with its light flickering over her beautiful skin wasn't helping matters. It only brought back erotic memories. As it was, he was barely holding on to his sanity with the tips of his fingernails.

Giving himself space to form his thoughts, he put two pieces of wood on the fire. Noelle quietly dried her hair with the heat from the flames.

"I really screwed up, didn't I?" he said at last. That, he noticed, got her attention. She stopped fussing with her hair. "I was wrong," he continued, "to accuse you of being deceitful. You only did what you felt was right."

"Why did you come to that conclusion now instead of weeks ago?"

Colin stifled a groan. "You're not going to make this easy, are you?"

"Why should I?"

Colin got up, paced before the fire. "The truth

is, listening to my father the other day has made me see how unfair I've been. And, like you said, maybe I was looking for an excuse, a way out. What we have is new for me. I've never been in love before. And I guess I didn't quite know how to handle it. Or whether I could trust it." This was the sorriest excuse for putting them both through hell, even to his own ears.

Noelle regarded him skeptically. "And you trust your emotions now?"

"Yeah." He had to figure out a way to make her believe him. Then maybe she'd forgive him for being a fool without making him grovel.

"And you know what the best thing was about being with you?" he continued.

She shook her head. The towel had slid to the floor revealing smooth brown shoulders. He itched to reach out to caress them before holding her in his arms. Instead, he forced his gaze to her eyes.

"With you I never had to be perfect. I didn't have to live up to what someone else wanted me to be. You accepted me for who I was. With you I can be me." At least she was listening. Just by gazing into her expressive eyes, he could tell she finally believed him. Only, when their eyes met, he was hit by a blast of heat so severe it nearly knocked him over. His entire being vibrated with wanting her.

Noelle shook her head. "After all this time you expect me to walk back into your arms as if nothing has occurred between us?"

His brain was so cloudy, he didn't think he was capable of coming up with another plausible excuse for acting like an idiot. "I expect you to follow your heart. What feels right for you."

For a while the only noise was the crackling of embers in the fire. Trixie gazed at them contentedly from her perch nearby.

"This certainly isn't the most romantic apology I've ever heard," she finally said.

He'd won. A boulder lifted from his chest. He felt as giddy as if one of his thoroughbreds had won the Kentucky Derby. Except this was so much more important.

Chapter 12

"Why didn't you just tell me you wanted romance? Can't let it be said I didn't give you exactly what you asked for."

"I'm not sure I'm ready to forgive you yet." At that moment Noelle seemed ambiguous about what she wanted.

"Then let me convince you." He knelt in front of her and gathered her into his arms. "We've been apart too long, baby. This is right."

Noelle felt a rush of happiness and hope so intense that she held on to Colin tightly to keep from falling flat on the floor. And then she saw him approaching her. She knew he was going to kiss her, expected it, but the splendor of his lips on hers took her breath away.

Her reserve shattered as he gently pulled her closer to him and took his time exploring her. He brushed his tongue over the seam of her lips and she opened her mouth to him, deepening the kiss.

She felt him repositioning himself between her legs. Her breasts pressed against his powerful chest, and his erection was against her soft stomach.

Giving in so quickly might be a mistake, but she wasn't going to contemplate it any longer. She was going to savor every delicious, passionate moment.

"Welcome home, sweetheart."

She laughed and he kissed her again, hotter and harder this time.

His hands moved languidly over her body. Her hands were all over him, as well, unbuttoning his shirt.

Colin felt as if the breath had been punched out of his lungs. But maybe he was rushing things. As much as he wanted to carry her upstairs and make love to her until they were both exhausted from it, he had to give in to her needs.

"Honey, if you'd rather wait…"

"Stop talking," she said on a breathless sigh.

His chuckle turned into a deep-throated groan when her tongue swiped over his nipple. He wanted to take his time pleasuring her. Wanted to wring every depth of passion out of her, but her hands were frantically peeling the clothes off him, caressing him in places designed to drive him crazy.

"Hold on, baby. I want to take it slow."

"Next time," she said with a breathy sigh.

Colin yanked down the straps of her top and her rounded breasts fell into his hands. A gourmet feast, he thought, as he lowered his head and ran his tongue over the globes before he suckled on the dark chocolate peaks.

He glanced up to her eyes and stroked her lips with his thumb before capturing them with his mouth once again. Then he was kissing her everywhere, her cheek, her neck her shoulder. He was a starving man before a feast and he wanted to devour all of her.

He ran his hand along the insides of her thighs.

"How long have I wanted to do this?"

"Probably as long as I've waited for you to come to your senses."

"Don't remind me, sweetheart." He lifted his head, looked into her eyes. "Maybe love makes you do stupid things."

"Love?"

"Yeah. What else could it be?" Slowly he undid the back of her top and it fell to the floor. He pulled her up and slid the bikini bottom down her smooth legs.

When Noelle gathered his erection in her hands and stroked him, he lost all control.

In seconds, they were on the carpet in front of the fire and he was inside her. Straining, he didn't move but gazed into her eyes.

"I love you, Noelle. Your name is like a song on my lips." Then he kissed her and they moved at a frantic pace as old as time. And when they climaxed, Colin thought he'd lost a part of himself, yet gained more.

Noelle was surprised when Carp stopped by Friday afternoon. He was dressed in black slacks and a new navy sweater.

"You look very nice, Carp."

He nodded. "Hope you don't mind. I used the shower in one of the counselor's cottages."

"I don't mind at all," Noelle said.

"I'm going to pick my kids up pretty soon. My ex is driving halfway to meet me. Give them a chance to spend the entire weekend with me for a change."

"I'm so happy for you."

"Yeah, I'm pretty happy, too. I've been beating that road to Baltimore in bad weather and good. They're looking forward to the trip, too," he said. "I've got things planned. Colin said I could bring them by the farm tomorrow. Maybe let them ride an old nag."

Noelle remembered her lessons with Mackenzie. It had been one of the highlights of her summer. "They'll enjoy that."

"He's a nice guy. Never looks down on me the way some people do. Well, I have to go. Wanted to let you know I wasn't going to be here the whole day."

"Enjoy your weekend with your children."

"I was wondering if maybe I could sign them up for that summer camp."

"I have room. We'll talk about it next week."

"All right. You have fun at your party."

Noelle's stomach was jumpy about meeting George's relatives. Would all of them feel as William felt, as if she were inheriting something that belonged to them?

She was on her way to her office when Trixie barked again. She knew by now that another car was coming up her drive. And to think that because she lived in the country she'd thought her life would be rather sedate.

She peeped out her curtain. It was George this time with an armful of photo albums. Noelle grabbed a coat and went outside to help him. Trixie ran to the bushes for a moment before she came back yapping.

"I was hoping you were home," George said. "I thought you'd like to look through these family albums. We can share some of the pictures."

"I'd love to see them." Once George was inside they got comfortable in front of the fireplace. She was grateful her dad had gotten her the cord of wood. At the rate she was going she'd use it all before March.

"Mackenzie kept an eye on you for the first few years. Even visited you and took pictures of you while he was at a convention in L.A. You didn't see him, though. He even wrote a letter to you after you contacted him, and he made a scrapbook and diary for you, telling you things about our lives. I've got pictures of your grandmother, too." His expression turned sad. "Wish you'd met her. She was a good woman. You remind me of her."

Noelle flipped the page. The album had pictures

of her during summer camp. Pictures of Mackenzie teaching her to ride. Pictures of her riding her bicycle when she was a little older.

"I found an insurance policy he left for you. I called the office. You should get the money before too long."

Insurance money was the last thing Noelle expected from Mackenzie.

"Some more things are in there. I'll let you look through them at your leisure."

"Thanks, George."

Standing, he stared at her for a moment. Then awkwardly he pulled her into his arms. She wrapped her arms around him.

"You've made me so happy," he said before he let her go.

Noelle watched him go. Many times she thought she was selfish for coming here interfering in his life. For the first time, she realized it was the very best thing she could have done. And whatever problems came from her decision in time could be worked out.

Noelle started leafing through the books. George had tucked in several envelopes. In one was a letter Mackenzie had written her years ago and never mailed. The second letter was dated the day after she'd contacted him. She read them both and cried.

* * *

The next day, around noon, Colin came into the house to grab a sandwich for lunch. He was feeling on top of the world. He'd found his way into Noelle's room around four-thirty that morning and had given her a grand wake-up call. On top of that, a couple of Diamond Spirit's offspring had won key races. George was renegotiating what they were charging for Diamond's stud fees.

Dreams do come true, Colin thought.

Leila was in the kitchen stirring something in a pot.

"A month ago I wouldn't have imagined George would be so happy," she said.

"The last few weeks have been good, haven't they?" Colin said.

"You've been pretty chipper lately."

Leila had a roundabout way of getting to her point.

"I only have a little time for lunch. Mind getting to the point, if it needs to be made at all?"

"Don't get sassy with me, young man. I knew you when."

"It's a crying shame for a grown man to be put in such a situation."

"You and Noelle look good together. Had me worried for a while," she said. "George lit into

William for bothering her. He's real protective of that girl."

"Don't worry. I'm not the big bad wolf who's going to knock her house down."

"Maybe she needs it knocked down." Leila chuckled. "Wolves aren't necessarily a bad thing."

"You're getting sassy, Leila. Where's my sandwich?"

"Just finding that out?" she asked. But she took her own good time getting to his lunch. "With these two properties joined, it'll make a nice farm."

"They make nice farms separately. We're doing okay on our own. I don't need Noelle for her land."

"Well, I wasn't saying that," she said in a huff. "But it wouldn't hurt. Still don't think it's a good idea for a woman to live out there alone like that."

Tired of the conversation, Colin said, "I'll make my own sandwich."

"Just hold your drawers," she said and finally got to work on his food.

He didn't need that advice from Leila. He'd already discovered what life was like without Noelle. With her was a thousand times better. But all this talk of properties was getting on his nerves. His father still hadn't spoken to him about the contracts. But at least George had started holding down his share of the work around the place.

Noelle waited impatiently for Casey in Salamanders. They were going to Tysons Corner to shop for dresses for the party after lunch. Noelle glanced at her watch just as Casey slid into a chair across from her.

"Sorry I'm late," she said. "I actually had a cordial conversation with Colin for a change. Things must be looking up with the two of you. For a while there, I thought I might need to find another job. He was a bear to work with."

"I'm sure his personality had nothing to do with me."

"Think again. Of course he's still out of sorts for losing that foal. They were really counting on that. The races this weekend might make a difference. Looking forward to the party next weekend?"

"A little nervous. It seems so much has happened lately my head's spinning."

"You'll be okay, Noelle. Who wouldn't like you?"

Noelle could name one person in particular.

"So, when will your brother be back?" Casey asked.

"He said next month for spring break but I'm not

counting on it. He usually goes to the beach in Florida." Why did Casey care? Noelle thought. Could Casey really like her brother? He was younger than she by at least a couple of years. But that wasn't a big thing any longer. He was certainly taken by her. And he asked about Casey every time Noelle called him.

"I'm going back to school in September," Casey told her. "I dropped out two years before I finished."

"Good for you."

"I figure we're too busy during breeding, but I can attend the fall semesters and summers." Casey glanced at her watch. "If we're going to shop today, we have to get a move on. You have to get a sexy number to wow Colin."

Colin had to watch the tape once more. He held his breath as he watched the race on the sports channel. Every time he saw it he felt the same jump in his chest. Diamond Spirit's colt won by a length. He'd won his last three races. And he wasn't the only one winning, though he stood out more than the others.

The multiple wins had doubled the price for Diamond Spirit's stud fees. Even now, Casey was booking sessions for Diamond Spirit. New mares were due to start arriving in four days. Not just any mare could mate with Diamond Spirit. He and George were working nonstop on checking out the mares' lineages. But Colin had stopped working for the day.

He wanted to celebrate with Noelle. Share the news with her.

Colin exploded into her house around six with a bottle of champagne. He picked her up and whirled her around in a circle.

"What's going on?" she asked, laughing. Trixie was dancing around, barking at the excitement.

"I can't believe it. A couple of Diamond Spirit's offspring have won some major races. His stud fees have risen to two hundred grand."

"You're kidding! He gets paid that much just to have sex?"

"Thoroughbred breeding is a lot of work. All kinds of things can go wrong, not to mention one misplaced kick from a mare can put Diamond out of business. We deserve double what we're getting." He shook his head. "George sure can pick a horse," he said.

"You knew that a long time ago. I'm glad something good is finally happening with him. I wish your granddad could see this day. But you're here, aren't you?"

Colin's smile was sad. He wished he could share this moment with his grandfather, too. "Yeah." Now more than ever he had to hold on to the farm. He'd have to e-mail his father about drawing up that contract. He was going to do everything in his power to make sure a Mayes continued what his grandfather had started all those years ago.

It was Saturday and just moments before the party was to begin. Colin was hanging around outside. He couldn't touch a thing in the house without Leila nearly rapping him on the fingers. Every time he'd tried to steal one of those tiny sandwiches, she'd hollered. So, although he was hungry, he'd left.

George was putting on quite a show, he'd even hired people to park cars. It was a formal affair and he tugged at his tux collar. The thing was about to strangle him to death.

He glanced upstairs at Noelle's room, wishing he could sneak in. She was still dressing. Hairdressers, manicure, pedicure—she and Casey had been yakking about it all week.

It would be the perfect time and place, in front of both her families—the Averys and the Greenwoods.

Maybe he'd propose at the party tonight. George had snuck out to the airport to pick up her family. Noelle was still in the dark about their arrival, though Colin knew she'd be happy to see them.

His dad's car was the first to arrive—a whole hour before the party. Colin's gut tightened. He wasn't in the mood for a fight tonight. He was trying to figure out a good time to propose to Noelle.

Instead of going to the house, Leander approached Colin.

"How are you, son?"

"Good," Colin said cautiously. He couldn't help but be wary. Nothing good had come from conversations with his dad lately.

Leander's perfectly fitted tux shouted money and status. He tucked his hands into his pockets. For once he seemed unsure of himself, which was counter to his character.

"Had some pretty good wins over the weekend, I see," Leander said.

Colin nodded, waiting for the older man to get to the point.

"I talked to George. Seems your stud fees doubled."

"Yeah."

He slid a hand into his inside breast pocket and

pulled out an envelope. He hit it against his hand a couple of times.

"You've been right about a few things. I've been unfair. Business hasn't been going as well as I've wanted it to in the last year. I knew some changes were called for and I was hoping to sell my share of the farm to make enough money to finance a new project."

Colin stood frozen into silence. Had his father sold the farm? God, no! His future was just flushed right down the drain.

"But for the last couple of weeks I've been considering other alternatives."

Colin's heart started beating again, but only a little. Did that mean he hadn't sold out? Colin didn't know what to think. His insides were twisted like a pretzel.

"So," Leander continued, "I've decided to give you half of my interest in the farm outright and sell you the other half prorated on what Dad paid."

Colin couldn't believe it. He was *giving* him half the farm?

"None of the other kids are interested in it. Dad wanted you to have it. He just didn't know how to do it without being unfair to the other kids. So here." He held out the envelope.

With shaky fingers, Colin took it. "I..." Colin

cleared the lump in his throat. In a million years he'd never expected his father to give him half the farm. "I can't believe it. Are you going to be able to pull your company out?"

"Yes, that's already in the works. Aaron and I had a long talk about what should be done. He's been nagging me to death to make changes the last couple of years. I never listened. I guess I felt the burden of the company was mine alone, instead of looking at it as a family endeavor. The boy has some good ideas. Guess we need some younger heads now and then to keep a fresh perspective."

"Thanks, Dad. I..."

"Believe it or not, I'm proud of you, son. Proud of what you've done for this farm. You deserve it." Leander then did something he hadn't done since Colin was a boy. He wrapped his arms around him and hugged him, then patted him on the shoulder and walked away.

Colin watched him. He still couldn't believe it. None of it. When Leander entered the house, Colin glanced at the contents of the envelope. It was a bill of sale for the farm at a rate and terms that he could pay on time without touching the money his grandfather had left him. More importantly, his father believed in him, approved of what he was doing.

Colin swallowed past the lump in his throat. He glanced at the mountains fading to darkness. Life couldn't get better than this. The only thing that would top it was for Noelle to agree to marry him. He didn't know how she'd feel about living in a house with two other people, but they'd have the upstairs to themselves. George never came up there. Leila's room was on the first floor, too.

Colin figured he could change one of the bedrooms into a den. His suite was more than twice the size of her bedroom, so they'd have enough room without cramping her style. If she didn't want to move there, he'd move in with her.

But first he had to convince her to marry him.

"Casey, my hair will not cooperate," Noelle moaned.

"Stop messing with it. It's perfect. Lord, Colin's going to lose his tongue when he sees you in that winter-white dress, girlfriend."

"You're the one who picked it out."

"And what a choice it is!" Casey said.

Noelle got her first glimpse of Casey in a lovely sleeveless gown that hugged her curves. "You're pretty sharp yourself."

Casey patted her hair. "Oh, this old thing?"

"Old thing, nothing."

"Well, we'll just see who I can latch on to at the party. A lot of money is coming here tonight. George sent invitations to everyone in the know. It's not just family. So we're going to see a lot of bigwigs."

Noelle stepped into her heels. "I could have gone a few more hours without hearing that."

"You don't have even a few minutes. George asked me to bring you downstairs now. So let's go."

"All right." Noelle took one last look in the mirror before she left with Casey. She almost felt like some fairy-tale princess as she descended the stairs.

Colin was standing at the foot. "My God, you're gorgeous," he breathed. And she believed him because he was looking at her as though he wanted to throw her over his shoulder and run away with her. "I'm scared to kiss you."

"You can make up for it tonight."

He held his arm out and she placed her hand in the crook of his elbow. "You can count on it," he said as he escorted her to the den.

And then she stopped, shocked.

"I can't believe it." She rushed across the room and flew into her parents' arms. She'd told them about the party but they'd made little of it. "I didn't know you were coming."

"George invited us," her mother said, looking gorgeous in a royal-blue gown. She'd kept her figure and was still beautiful. Her dad stood tall and elegant in his tux. Even Greg wore a tux. He and Casey were standing apart talking.

"Mom, I want you to meet Colin Mayes."

Colin stepped forward. "Pleased to meet you, ma'am." There were greetings all around before guests began to arrive, and Noelle was thrown into the thick of things. She spent most of the beginning of the night by George's side. Most of his relatives seemed quite pleased for him, even William's mother, which surprised her.

Noelle couldn't help noticing that Colin was particularly happy about something. Especially given that before the party he was griping about having to wear a tux.

And didn't he look great in it? She was thinking of fun ways to get it off him later on, when her mother approached her.

"How are you handling all this?" Harriet Greenwood asked.

"It's overpowering," Noelle said.

"Colin doesn't seem to be able to keep his eyes off you. So, what's going on?"

Noelle felt her face heat. "We're dating."

Her mother nodded. "Franklin hasn't stopped frowning since he brought you into the room."

"Daddy hasn't liked any of my dates."

Harriet gazed fondly at her handsome husband. "He can be a little overprotective, but he'll get used to it. By the looks of your young man, he's here for the duration."

Noelle glanced at Colin. She certainly hoped so.

"Who's that surly gentleman over there? He looks familiar."

Noelle frowned. "He's William, George's nephew."

"He doesn't seem to be too pleased about you."

"He isn't. I think my arrival put a damper on some of his plans. It's a long story. I'll tell you about it later," she said as the front door crashed open.

"There's a fire down the road," one of the valets shouted. "Call the fire department."

They ran outside. "Looks like your place," Colin said, retrieving his cell phone and calling the fire department at the same time he shrugged out of his coat and placed it on Noelle's shoulders.

Her heart jumped into her throat. Everything she owned was in the house.

Colin held her hand as they drove to the house. But when they pulled up in the yard and saw that the house wasn't on fire, some of her panic receded. He kept driving toward the camp.

God, please don't let it be the dorm, she prayed. There was no way she could replace it in time to open for the summer.

Great clouds of billowing smoke gushed into the air. The acrid smell reached them before they made it to the camp.

It was only the little cottage, thank God, but it would still present a problem if it spread to the other buildings. Fire had already engulfed it, sparks were flying into the air.

She heard sirens in the distance, but she doubted they'd be able to save the building.

When they arrived, the crews worked efficiently, wetting down the other structures to keep the fire from spreading before they started on the flaming building. But Noelle already knew the cottage was lost. The cold had gone through her like a chilled wind. How could this have happened?

Colin felt helpless. He glanced up to see William talking to someone. As much as the man hated Noelle, Colin didn't understand why he was even here.

Hours later the firemen questioned Noelle about the repairs being made on the building. It was two in the morning before they finally made it home.

A bedraggled group hauled themselves into George's house.

"I wouldn't be surprised if your carpenter hadn't left that heater on," William said when everyone was sitting around.

"He's very careful," Noelle countered.

"He's a drunk."

"He hasn't taken a drink in weeks. He doesn't drink on the job," she said. "And most of his problems have been cleared up. So it wasn't him."

"Just a suggestion," William said, backing off.

"How did you know he used a heater in there?" Colin asked. "I'm around all the time and I didn't know that."

"What?"

"The heater. How did you know he used one? You haven't been there, have you?"

"All carpenters use heaters in winter. Doesn't take a genius to know that."

"He wasn't working in that building," Noelle said. "He just patched it up a little. Just used it to dress and eat sometimes to get away from the dust in the other buildings. So how did you know?"

"I don't remember seeing you early on," Colin said to William. "You arrived late."

William stood his ground. "I'm not going to let you grill me like a criminal."

"Do you hate her that much?" George asked. "You never were going to get the farm. If Noelle hadn't come along, I would have left it to Colin. I knew you would sell it and I didn't want that. I wanted this farm to survive. And I knew Colin would see that it would." George swiped a hand over his face. "You burned that girl's building down, didn't you?" He sat down tiredly. "You know this would just about kill your mother. How could you do such a thing?"

"I didn't—"

"Stop the lying," George said. "It's written all over your face. You've brought nothing but grief from the time you heard about Noelle. I knew your character before. I just never thought you'd stoop this low."

It took two days for the smoke from the fire to clear. George sent over a crew to clean up the debris.

"You don't have to watch this, sweetheart," Colin said, standing at the kitchen counter in her house. "I'll take care of it."

"I want to be part of it. This place meant so much to my grandparents. I don't understand how someone could be so vicious."

"There's evil in the world, you know that. But we don't have to let it touch us."

"We can't stop it."

"No, we can't. But it can't stop us from living a good life. I love you, Noelle. No matter what goes on outside, we'll always be strong. Together. If you marry me."

"What?"

Colin sighed. He hadn't meant to ask her like this. He was dressed in grungy clothes with the scent of fire and horse on him. This wasn't how he wanted to propose.

"I wanted to make it a special occasion," he said. "With wine and roses. I wanted us all dressed up and...I know this isn't romantic." He stroked the side of her face. "And I know how you love romance. But I love you, sweetheart. I want to marry you, to spend the rest of my life with you."

Noelle screeched and hauled herself into his arms, linking her arms around his neck. "You're wrong. If this isn't romance, what is?"

"You're the expert," Colin said, not about to argue.

"Yes. I'll marry you."

"You've made my day, my week, my year." He grabbed her and kissed her until her stomach growled. "Guess I'd better let you eat."

"Guess you'd better," she said. She'd set out the soup and sandwiches Leila had sent over and, sitting side by side, they ate at the island.

"When are your parents going back?"

"Sunday." Greg had left already to return to school. "I'm glad Dad and George are getting along. I was worried in the beginning."

"George has a way of winning people over. He and your dad smoked cigars and played poker all night. Leila's complaining as usual."

"Yeah, Mom had a lot to say about that marathon poker night. It's going to be tough keeping Dad away now. But Mom doesn't complain too much."

"George is planning to take him to some of the races."

"Gregory, too. He actually called me last night to tell me George is taking him to a race during spring break. You have to understand that my brother doesn't call. I have to call him."

Colin chuckled. "You know how guys are."

"I expect you to be more considerate."

"Yes, ma'am." Colin ate for a moment. "Has the thought crossed your mind that there could be other children by Mackenzie?"

"At first, until Mom told me he wasn't a regular

donor. He did this exclusively for Mom and Dad. So I'm it."

"So." He wrapped an arm around her waist, kissed her neck. "When do we get married? I don't like long engagements. And with your parents around, I won't be able to sneak over."

"Hmm," Noelle said, leaning into his kisses. "Weddings take time to plan."

Colin moaned. "George put the party together in a couple weeks."

"Weddings are different, trust me. It takes longer than that to find a gown."

"I trust you, baby." Suddenly a gleam came into his eyes. "Think we can have a little fun before your parents get back?"

She ran her hands across the bulge in his pants. "I'm game if you are."

ALWAYS *Means* FOREVER

DEBORAH FLETCHER MELLO

Despite her longtime attraction to Darwin Tollins, Bridget Hinton rejects a casual fling with the notorious playboy. But when Darwin seeks her legal advice, he discovers a longing he's never known. How can he revise Bridget's opinion of him?

Available the first week of June wherever books are sold.

www.kimanipress.com

Can she handle the risk...?

daring devotion

ELAINE OVERTON

Author of FEVER

Andrea Chenault has always believed she could live with the fear every firefighter's wife knows. But as her wedding to Calvin Brown approaches, she's tormented by doubts as several deadly fires seem to be targeting the man she loves.

Available the first week of June wherever books are sold.

KIMANI ROMANCE

www.kimanipress.com

KPEO0220607

Love is always better...

The Second Time Around

Angie Daniels

Visiting her hometown, Brenna Gathers runs into Jabarie Beaumont, the man who jilted her at the altar years ago. Convinced by his father Brenna was a gold digger, Jabarie never got her out of his system. Now he's on a mission to win Brenna's heart a second time.

Available the first week of June wherever books are sold.

KIMANI ROMANCE

www.kimanipress.com

From five of today's hottest names in women's fiction…

CREEPIN'

Superlative stories of paranormal romance.

MONICA JACKSON
& FRIENDS

Alpha males, sultry beauties and lusty creatures confront betrayal and find passion in these super sexy tales of the paranormal with an African-American flavor.

Featuring new stories by L.A. Banks, Donna Hill, J.M. Jeffries, Janice Sims and Monica Jackson.

Coming the first week of June
wherever books are sold.

KIMANI PRESS™

www.kimanipress.com

KPMJ0600607

Acclaimed author
Adrianne Byrd

Blue Skies

Part of Arabesque's At Your Service military miniseries.

Fighter pilot Sydney Garret was born to fly. No other thrill came close—until Captain James Colton ignited in her a reckless passion that led to their short-lived marriage. When they parted, Sydney knew fate would somehow reunite them. But no one imagined it would be a matter of life or death....

"Byrd proves once again that she's a wonderful storyteller."
—*Romantic Times BOOKreviews* on
THE BEAUTIFUL ONES

Coming the first week of June
wherever books are sold.

ARABESQUE®

www.kimanipress.com

KPAB0120607